FRIDAY I'M IN LOVE

ALSO BY CAMRYN GARRETT

Full Disclosure

Off the Record

FRIDAY I'M IN LOVE

CAMRYN GARRETT

PENGUIN BOOKS

PENGUIN BOOKS

UK | USA | Canada | Ireland | Australia
India | New Zealand | South Africa

Penguin Books is part of the Penguin Random House group of companies
whose addresses can be found at global.penguinrandomhouse.com

www.penguin.co.uk
www.puffin.co.uk
www.ladybird.co.uk

Penguin
Random House
UK

First published in the USA by Alfred A. Knopf, an imprint of
Random House Children's Books 2023
This edition published in Great Britain by Penguin Books 2023
001

Text copyright © Camryn Garrett, 2023
Illustrations copyright © Erick Dávila, 2023
Interior art used under license from Shutterstock

'Friday I'm in Love'
Words and music by Robert Smith, Simon Gallup,
Paul S. Thompson, Boris Williams, and Perry Bamonte.
Copyright © 1992 by Fiction Songs Ltd.
All rights in the United States and Canada administered
by Universal Music-MGB Songs. International copyright secured.
All rights reserved. Reprints by permission of Hal Leonard LLC

The moral right of the author and illustrator has been asserted

Text design by Michelle Crowe
Set in 9.5/16.15pt Calisto MT Pro.
Printed and bound in Great Britain by Clays Ltd, Elcograf S.p.A.

The authorized representative in the EEA is Penguin Random House Ireland,
Morrison Chambers, 32 Nassau Street, Dublin D02 YH68

A CIP catalogue record for this book is available from the British Library

ISBN: 978-0-241-56274-1

All correspondence to:
Penguin Books
Penguin Random House Children's
One Embassy Gardens, 8 Viaduct Gardens, London SW11 7BW

To Lingeringlillies, for showing me what type of queer woman I wanted to be without even knowing my name.

FRIDAY I'M IN LOVE

Dressed up to the eyes

It's a wonderful surprise

To see your shoes and your spirits rise

Throwing out your frown

And just smiling at the sound

And as sleek as a shriek,

Spinning 'round and 'round

Always take a big bite

It's such a gorgeous sight

To see you in the middle of the night

You can never get enough

Enough of this stuff

It's Friday

I'm in love!

—'FRIDAY I'M IN LOVE' BY THE CURE

APRIL

CHAPTER 1

It's Mom's idea to drive me to Naomi's Sweet Sixteen.

If you're thinking it's because I can't drive, the San Diego Department of Motor Vehicles would disagree—it doesn't matter that I had to take the test three times. I have my license. And yet, I still barely get to drive when I want to. Like right about now.

"You know," I say. "If *I'd* had a Sweet Sixteen, Naomi would have driven to it by herself."

"Mahalia."

Mom presses her lips tightly together. She never takes her eyes off the road when she's driving, so I can roll my eyes all I want and get away with it. But honestly, it's just not as fun when she's not looking at me, so I stare down at my lap instead. Naomi's gift is at my feet, shoved in a sparkly bag we got from the dollar store. It's just a dress from Forever 21, but I had to use a good amount of gas money to buy it. I hope it doesn't look as cheap as it feels.

"We've discussed this *multiple* times," Mom adds. "There wasn't any money for you to have a party. Not this year."

Don't be a brat, don't be a brat—

"But you *said* I could have one," I say, folding my arms.

1

"Remember? You said I could have a gigantic party when I turned sixteen because you never got to have one."

"When you were *six*," Mom fires back. "Things were different when you were six."

I duck my head again, chagrined. Mom is right. Things *were* different when I was six—we had way less money. It's taken her a long time to get us to where we are. But sometimes I want more. And I always feel like a total asshole about it.

A strand of hair blows into my mouth and I spit it out. The windows are down because Mom is anti-AC, and I like the way the breeze blows my hair everywhere. It's not coarse enough to stick up in an Afro, but not soft enough for me to wear like white girls do, so it's sort of this frizzy mop that I braid every night to keep contained and take out every morning. At least I had the sense to wear a headband.

"Anyway, a girl doesn't need a party," Mom says. "There are bills to pay, Mahalia. Rent and electric and heat and food, all these bills. Would you rather have had your party and then starved for the rest of the year?"

I mean, it would've been nice to have the party.

"It doesn't sound so bad," I finally settle on, trying to coax a laugh out of her. "We wouldn't be out on the street or anything. We could live with Dad."

Mom makes this sound like *pshh*.

"Okay," I say. Maybe not the best joke. When Dad and his girlfriend had my younger half sister, Reign, he "forgot" to pay child support for six months. I doubt he'd feed us for a year. "But I'm sure it wouldn't have been a big deal. You always say the Lord provides, right?"

"Not for foolish things," she says. "The Lord provides us with what we need."

"Does He?" I try to make my voice light, but it's hard. "Then why don't we have a house? Or a college fund for me? Or money for you to go back to college?"

Mom's hands tighten on the steering wheel.

"God isn't a genie. You know that," she says. "You don't rub a Bible and wait for three wishes."

I snort. She looks at me out of the corner of her eye and smiles a little. For a second, I think it's over, we've moved past the whole *God* thing. But then—

"The Lord gave us bodies to work," she says. "He led me to the nursing home job when I—when *we*—needed it most. He gave you the brains to find a great scholarship for next fall. The Lord helps those who help themselves. Remember that, okay?"

I kind of hate talking about God with Mom, mostly because it seems like the rules change all the time; from person to person, even from Sunday to Sunday at the church we've been going to, since I was little, for the past few years. Everything about it feels too convenient. The Lord will provide, but not too much. The Lord forgives us for our sins, but sinning is bad and we should never do it.

At church, when Pastor Patrick says, "The devil is *alive* in this country today," Mom's "Amen" is just as loud as the word of God. She always says the devil is the cause of temptation and the one who tries to lead us away from the Lord and that's why she got pregnant when she was seventeen. Not because Dad was convincing and Mom was horny.

Part of me wants to say *Mom* is the reason why she got that job, not God. But I know that would just start a fight. Instead, I reach for the radio. She smacks my hand away and switches on one of her Christian hip-hop CDs. I groan dramatically.

"Oh please," Mom says over the funky beats. "I know you love this."

Some of the songs *are* catchy. But then I have Bible verses stuck in my head for the rest of the day and feel like a heathen for not believing in them.

Thank God the big, ornate columns of the restaurant are coming up on the left—an all-white building right on the water. Gigantic windows look out over the beach. It's the type of venue only Naomi's parents could afford. The type of venue I wish I could've had for my nonexistent party.

But it doesn't matter anymore. It's too late for me to have a Sweet Sixteen and there's no such thing as a Sweet Seventeen. The next-best big party to look forward to is, like, a wedding or funeral.

Mom stops in front of the restaurant and I'm pretty sure I'm gaping. There are people dressed up in uniforms, taking coats and parking cars. It's crazy.

"Be good," Mom says, pinching my cheek. "I don't want to hear that you were being disrespectful to Mr. and Mrs. Sanders. Understand?"

I stick my tongue out at her. She's mostly kidding—I'm at Naomi's house all the time and I'm pretty sure I see her parents more than I see my own mother, but I don't say that. It's not her fault that the nursing home gives her these insane hours. She's wearing her scrubs now, and for a second, my brain flashes forward, seeing the way she slowly shuffles into our apartment after a twelve-hour shift like she hasn't had the chance to sit all day.

"Mahalia?"

People dressed in high heels and suit jackets are already heading inside. I barely recognize any of the faces, but I'm pretty sure *they* don't shop at Forever 21. My spine stiffens. This isn't going to be like hanging out at Naomi's house after school.

Mom nudges me forward.

"Be good," she says again as I open the door. "I love you."

"Bye, Mom." I force myself to swallow. "Love you, too."

I step out of her beat-up car and don't look back.

CHAPTER 2

When Naomi and her parents first started planning her party, I was so excited, it could've been my own. I wanted to go with her to try on dresses and pick out invitations and talk about what music she'd play. Along the way, I guess I forgot that I wouldn't be the only guest here.

Naomi is my best friend, but she's a lot better at the *social* part of friendship. I know a lot of people because we go to school together, but they're not exactly *friends*—more like people I'd be lab partners with.

This room is full of potential lab partners. Naomi has friends of different races and genders and ages. There are round tables draped in white cloths where people nibble on appetizers. Then there's the big wooden dance floor, where a few brave souls are trying to get things going.

I plant myself at a table and stay there, even as more people migrate to the dance floor. I'm sitting with strangers: an older woman with hair like a bees' nest, a married couple, and a girl I recognize from school. Maybe every ten minutes, there's a Naomi spotting, and I can't keep my eyes off her dress.

6

I was there when she bought it with her mom—I still remember the saleswoman gushing, using terms like *plunging V-neck bodice* and *natural waist* that didn't really make sense to me. One thing was—still is—easy to understand: Naomi looks beautiful. The dress is long and lavender. If I ignore the spaghetti straps and the lace-up back, I could totally see Naomi hitching up her skirts and running through the countryside after some forbidden lover in a Jane Austen movie.

I try to wave to her, but she only notices me once. She's like a queen with hundreds of subjects swarming around her at once, appearing genuinely excited to talk to aunts and uncles and cousins.

Sigh.

"Mahalia!"

I jump at the booming voice. Behind me, Mr. Sanders is looking down with a grin. His forehead is sweaty and there's a dark spot on his blue dress shirt. I can't help but smile back at him.

"I've been looking everywhere for you," he says. "Why aren't you dancing?"

"Oh," I say, glancing at the dance floor. There are little kids chasing each other and squealing. "I was. I just, uh, needed a break."

He doesn't even call me out on the obvious lie. Instead, he practically yanks me out of my seat and in for a hug. I rest against his shoulder before realizing it's sweaty, too. It's hot in here, like the AC can't keep up with all the people dancing and singing on the dance floor. Naomi hasn't done any of the traditional Sweet Sixteen stuff—no court, no fancy shoes, no speeches. The only thing that's happened is a lot of good food and a shit ton of dancing.

Mr. Sanders rocks us back and forth. "Are you sure the musical selection is up to your standards?"

I frown before I can help it.

"I don't know what the DJ is doing," I say. "He should just play, like, classic hits. Half of the people here don't know any Doja Cat songs."

And rightfully so, honestly.

"Ah, that's my girl," he says. The grin stretches even wider. "I told Naomi we should play something old-school, maybe a little Luther Vandross—"

"Oh no, Mr. S," I say. "There's no way she was gonna go for that."

He laughs. I don't think he's drunk, just happy. It's almost odd to see a parent so happy. Sometimes Mom is *okay,* but I don't know if I've ever seen her happy.

"I hate to see you sitting here all alone," he says, sobering. "I'm sure Naomi would love to hang out with you."

"Oh yeah," I say, glancing behind me. "I was trying to find her, but she has a ton of people to talk to. It's fine. Seriously. I'll track her down later."

Familiar piano notes catch my attention. My head snaps to the dance floor. Stevie Wonder's "Don't You Worry 'Bout a Thing" filters through the speakers. All the Black adults have migrated to the center of the room, swaying and cheering. My hips start moving softly to the beat. It's sort of impossible not to move to Stevie Wonder.

Naomi's mom is getting down with another woman near the DJ's station. Mrs. Sanders looks like she could still be in college, even though she has three kids and is a big fancy lawyer. She giggles with her friend like she's in high school. Suddenly, she looks so much like Naomi that my heart clenches. I want to dance with my best friend, too. Not her dad.

"You're welcome to mingle with Mrs. Sanders and me," he offers, twirling me. "We're trying to figure out how to dance to this music together."

"No, I'm fine," I say, shrugging away from him. "I was actually headed to the bathroom. Thank you, though. I'll catch up with you later."

"Sure thing." He smiles. Mr. Sanders is always smiling. I wonder what it's like to be genuinely pleased with every aspect of your life. "I'll see you later, Mahalia."

He says my name the way it's supposed to be said, all full of soul and swing. Mom makes it sound flat and businesslike.

I ask a waiter where the bathroom is before heading down the hallway. The late-afternoon sun streams through the high windows, lighting the way to the bathroom at the end of the hall. I'm not wearing a long princess dress like Naomi, but a cute skirt. My legs feel bare.

There are usually a ton of women in public bathrooms, but I'm surprised to find this one empty. I glance at myself in one of the mirrors. I did my makeup at home with YouTube tutorials; usually I get Naomi to help me out, but she was busy getting herself ready for the party. When I left the house, I could've walked straight out of a prom picture, but now my face looks like I've sweat almost everything off. And I didn't even *dance*. It's not fair.

"Do you need some help?"

I turn my head. It's a light-skinned Black girl who may or may not be mixed. Short, messy curls frame her head like a crown and a million brown freckles crowd her cheeks. There's something serious about her brown eyes, like she's studying me, but there's a soft smile on her lips. I don't think I've ever seen her at school before. If I had, I definitely would've noticed.

Because I'm *so* articulate around pretty girls, I choke out, "What?"

"You were touching your face." She steps forward, close enough that I can feel the warmth of her arm against mine. "Like you were worried about your makeup?"

"Oh." I feel like I can't breathe. There's a slight accent to her words, but I can't tell where it's from. "Yeah. I was— It's hot."

God. It's getting worse the more I talk. I just don't think I can stop. If I do, she might leave, and I want her to stay as long as possible.

"Here." She reaches into the small pink purse at her side. "Easiest just to wipe it off at this point."

She pulls out a bag of makeup wipes. I stand there, not moving, just watching. I want to say something flirty or funny, but there's nothing in my brain. Her purse closes with a click.

"It doesn't look bad," she says, eyes roaming over my shakily applied liner and blush. I'm frozen. "But I still think it's an awful idea to party when you're worried about your makeup the entire time. What do you think?"

"Uh," I say. "Sure?"

Her hand, covered with the small white sheet, hovers near my cheek.

"May I?"

I nod, probably too eagerly. I don't even know this girl's name, but she's so close to me, and I can't stop looking at her. She presses the wipe against my cheek and dabs gently. I watch her dark eyebrows as they furrow in concentration. Her touch is warm. Every part of my body is warm.

"There," she says, smacking her lips together. "Perfect."

She totally is. And she's all I can think about for the rest of the night—when I'm dancing to "Before I Let Go" with Naomi's dad, when I sneak a little champagne while the adults aren't looking, when I steal glances at her across the dance floor . . . She dances like a white woman in a commercial for some questionable medication, tossing her head back and laughing at the ceiling. I want to know why she's so happy. How long has she known Naomi? Did she find the champagne, too?

But by the time I've worked up the nerve to walk over, Naomi finally appears, sweaty and a little red and grinning like she has a secret.

"*There* you are," she says. "I've been looking for you everywhere."

She grips my arms, swinging them from side to side. At some point during the night, she acquired a tiara, and it rests on top of her head like it's been there all her life.

"Dude," I say, a laugh in my voice as I squeeze her arms. "I've been here. Have you been chasing after Cody or something?"

I'm just teasing—I haven't actually seen Naomi with Cody tonight. He's this geeky white boy Naomi has had a crush on forever. They're pretty similar—both at the top of our class and in every after-school activity.

Naomi giggles. Oh, she *definitely* found the champagne.

"Not *yet*. But the night is still *perfect*," she says, practically whispering in my ear. "Don't you think?"

My chest feels fluttery, partially from the drink and partially from the dancing. I feel like I could dance all night and not think about who was looking at me. I can't remember the last time I felt this way. We're standing so close, our cheeks bump together when I nod. Naomi giggles again.

"Wait," I say. "You know what else is perfect?"

I turn back to where I last saw the stranger doing her pharma ad white girl dance. But she's gone. It's like there's a hole on the dance floor.

"What's perfect?" Naomi says, squeezing my arm to get my attention.

Did I imagine what happened in the bathroom? Does the girl even exist? Is she really as fantastic as I thought, or am I just a little too tipsy on this party?

"Um," I say, turning back to Naomi. "The playlist."

"God, Mahalia." Naomi rolls her eyes. "Shut up and dance."

Then she pulls me toward the middle of the dance floor. Even when the DJ gives in and plays a Doja Cat song, when all the girls from school swarm the dance floor and it feels like I could dance all night, a small part of me is still thinking about the gentleness of her hand against my cheek. Even if my brain embellished the moment, fleshed it out into something it wasn't, the memory is warm and soft in my mind, just like her touch.

CHAPTER 3

School is pretty much the bane of my existence, but I'm actually, surprisingly, good at history. It's been my favorite subject since middle school. My teacher this year can be pretty annoying, though. And it's hard to go back to school on Monday after Naomi's Sweet Sixteen weekend.

I'm still a little high from the feeling of seeing that girl when Mr. Willis starts passing packets back. Danny, an annoying white boy, is in the middle of banging his drumsticks against his desk. You'd think he was a member of marching band or something, but no. Apparently, he just picked it up over the summer. Now all he does is bang the stupid drumsticks against his desk or the floor or the wall—and we all have to suffer.

"Danny," Mr. Willis says. "*Please* stop so I may think."

Danny pauses, drumsticks hovering above the wood-patterned linoleum of his desk. Mr. Willis lets out a painful sigh, rubbing at his temples, before his eye catches something else.

"Jacob," he says sternly, eyeing one of the students in the front row. "Food away."

"But, Mr. W," Jacob, an Asian kid with bleached-blond hair, groans. "It's just an orange and—"

"You know the rules." Mr. Willis continues passing packets back. "Now, we've already talked about your project, but I'll reiterate for the poor notetakers in the room. Each group will create a lesson plan centered around a topic we won't be able to fully cover in class—examples may include, but are not limited to, Reagan and conservatism, migration and immigration, and challenges of the twenty-first century. Although these topics are less likely to appear on the AP exam, it's important for you to be aware of *all* of US history, not just what happens to be included on a test. You will present your lesson to the class in a month's time, and submit a paper on what you've learned."

He pauses meaningfully, but it's lost on the rest of the class. My classmates are buzzing the way everyone does whenever a teacher announces a group project.

"I know you are used to forming your own groups in class," he says. "But this time, *I'll* be picking your groups for this project."

The entire class groans. Mr. Willis nods his head, like he was expecting this.

"I can't help but notice how you all pick the same partners each time," he says. "And that's not the point of group projects. The point is to expand your horizons. Meet someone new. Use your skills to . . ."

I start tuning him out then. I'm just about to read one of the little sidebars in our textbook for fun—that's how bored Mr. Willis makes me—when the door swings open. My eyes dart up and my jaw practically drops. It's not just someone coming back from the bathroom or another teacher asking to borrow a stapler. It's *her.* The girl from Naomi's party.

Her hair is pulled up in space buns, which is the cutest thing ever, and there seem to be even more freckles on her face than there were in that bathroom. She's wearing Birkenstocks—is she a hippie? I've generally only seen white people with dreads wear Birkenstocks, but they seem to *fit her.* Like this is just who she is—not a trend she's following.

She holds a binder close to her chest and has a tentative smile on her face. She takes a step into the room. Immediately, everyone is staring at her.

Before anyone can say a word, Danny yells out, "Babe! I lost you!"

Then he does a little drum solo. The girl blushes and tucks a strand of hair behind her ear, and the rest of the class breaks out into laughter. I'd normally roll my eyes. But right now? The word *babe* is bouncing around my brain. Danny wouldn't call her *babe* for no reason. As annoying as he is, I don't think he's that weird or creepy.

Which must mean—

"Siobhan!" Mr. Willis says. "Everyone, let's give a warm welcome to our new student, all the way from Ireland!"

He claps loudly and the class follows his lead with lukewarm applause. My hands feel frozen. *Siobhan.* That's her name. But as she sits in an empty desk near Danny, grabbing his hand, it's hard not to put it all together. Somehow, this girl started dating Danny before enrolling at our school.

Danny? *Him,* of all people?

I guess there's technically nothing *wrong* with him. He's average-looking—blond hair, blue eyes, tanned skin from being out in the sun so much. All he ever wears to school are T-shirts emblazoned with the school mascot (the Panthers) or his jersey, even though football season has been over since the fall. He has tons of friends who all sound, dress, and look like him. And then there's the whole drumming thing . . .

She could do a million times better.

"Groups, groups!" Mr. Willis picks up a piece of paper from his desk. "Jack, Isabel, and Sean in group one. Morgan, Jeremy, and Parker in group two. Danny, Siobhan, and Mahalia in group three."

My heart seems to stop beating when Siobhan turns to look at me. For a second, her smile is shy, but then recognition flickers in her eyes.

"It's you!" she says, turning her desk toward me. "From the party. Are you one of Naomi's friends?"

Danny's eyes dart between the two of us before he turns his desk, too.

"What party, babe?" he says to Siobhan, even though he's looking at me with something like an awkward smile. "The thing you went to this weekend?"

Everyone in the class is turning their desks, making little triangles, but these two have spared me the trouble by pointing their desks toward me. I wish I could push Danny into another group. Instead, I tap my pencil against the front page of our packet.

"It was a Sweet Sixteen," Siobhan says, leaning so she's practically sitting in Danny's lap. One of her hands starts absentmindedly playing with the gold chain around his neck. "I've never been to one before, but it was so fun. And I got to meet a new friend. Remind me of your name again?"

I want to look away—this image of them, sitting together like *that,* seems way too intimate for a classroom—but I don't want to be antisocial, either.

"Mahalia," I say. I should probably say something else, something cool and fun and spunky, but all my words seem to be clogged at the back of my throat. "My name's Mahalia Harris."

"Nice to meet you, Mahalia Harris." She reaches over and places her hand on top of mine. "I'm Siobhan Davidson."

I stare down at her hand, shocked by how tender it feels. Like we've known each other for years. Normally, I might think this was weird, like something my mom would do. I might flinch at the way she called me her friend, even though we barely just met. But right now I'm honestly just grateful she's paying attention to me.

"Everyone in their seats, please," Mr. Willis calls from his desk. "Their *own* seats."

Siobhan slides back into her own desk, cheeks still pink, but Danny places a hand on her thigh. They smile at each other—sweet and cute and disgusting.

"Babe," Danny says, opening his textbook with a loud thump. "Do you want me to drive you to your shift today?"

"That would be great," she says, rolling up her sleeves. A few bangles rest on her right wrist. "I was thinking—"

Her jaw opens wide, and the loudest yawn I've ever heard cuts through all the chatter in the classroom. Even Mr. Willis looks up from his desk and over at her. Siobhan places her hand over her mouth, cheeks reddening.

"Wow." I can't help but snicker. "History isn't *that* boring."

Siobhan draws in her lips, but her gaze is playful.

Danny snickers—why is he snickering? We aren't friends. Siobhan smiles, revealing a dimple in her cheek. Fuck. Did she have that dimple before? How dark was the light in the bathroom?

"Shiv is the biggest night owl," he says, wrapping his arm around her like they aren't sitting *right* next to each other. "You should see the type of trouble she gets into."

I hope he doesn't mean sex. God, *ew.*

"Really?" I know my eyebrows are probably up to my hairline, but I try my best to play it cool. "Um, when did you get here? From Ireland, I mean?"

"About a month ago. I was finishing up classwork online." Siobhan tucks a strand of hair behind her ear and stares down at the textbook, shifting in her seat. "So what topic do you think—"

She yawns again. It's not as loud as her first one, but twice as long. I try my best not to stare at her. Not to think about her and Danny doing whatever it is they do at night.

The thing about liking girls is that I don't want to be a creep. In most of the movies and shows I've seen, guys are the ones who like girls, and they're almost always weird about it. They stalk the girls or act like a girl they spoke to once suddenly belongs to them. They're territorial. Overbearing.

I don't want to be any of those things. I just want to sit close to Siobhan. I want to hear the lilt of her voice, look at her dimple, count the freckles on her face. I want to know what her favorite TV show is. If she likes coffee or tea. What she did on the weekends before she came here. I want to know everything about her.

But most of all, I want her to stop dating Danny. Which is ridiculous—Danny may be an annoying boy who has nothing important to say, but it's Siobhan's choice to date him. Not mine. And yet, I can't help but feel like she's out of his league. Which I hate. I sound like a weird middle-aged guy going after a younger girl in a rom-com written by a man.

Ugh.

"Mahalia?"

I glance up. Siobhan and Danny are staring at me with matching expressions. Which I also *hate*. She's been here, what, a week? How have they been together long enough to sync their expressions?

"I'm making a group chat," Siobhan says slowly, like I might not understand. "Can I have your number?"

Danny's drumsticks have reappeared. He taps slowly, methodically, like he's counting down—to what, I have no idea.

"Sure," I say, leaning forward. "Can I see your phone?"

CHAPTER 4

After school, I'm at Naomi's house, because I'm always at Naomi's house.

Maybe that's because it has air conditioning, which is really helpful when you're in Southern California. There's also Naomi's family. Her parents work a lot, but not nearly as much as my mom. One of them is always around for dinner. It's so weird.

They live in a big house with a kitchen that looks like it belongs on HGTV and there are enough rooms for everyone to have their own. Markus, Naomi's older brother, goes to Howard and her younger sibling, Cal, goes to this school where everyone calls their teachers by their first names. Again: so weird.

"Hey, Cal," I say, dumping my backpack by the front door. "How's it going?"

"Fine," they say, barely looking up from a book. "I'm up to my fortieth book this school year. I'm going to be the kid with the most in the entire school and then I get a prize."

"Wow."

It's Monday, so I can barely even process that sentence, especially after a full day of school. I glance over at Naomi, but she's moved on and into the living room.

"Is that after all the Harry Potter books?"

"Mahalia." Cal fixes me with a stare like I'm a little kid. "J. K. Rowling is transphobic. We have to stand up for trans rights."

"Right."

I turn away from the kitchen table. Mom never let me read the Harry Potter books because of the witchcraft. I guess she had good foresight.

"Try Percy Jackson," I say, grabbing an orange and heading toward the stairs. "There's like a million spin-offs and those books are my shit. Naomi, I'm going upstairs!"

All the bedrooms are up on the second floor, but you can see the ground floor from up here, which used to be a lot of fun and very helpful for spying on Markus's friends when we were younger.

I want a house like this, but I'm never going to be an engineer or a lawyer like Mr. and Mrs. Sanders, so I doubt it'll happen.

"Are you in my room?" Naomi calls from downstairs. "Hold on, I'm grabbing snacks! Don't start anything without me!"

Naomi's room hasn't changed much since we were little. She took down the posters of the Jonas Brothers and One Direction, but otherwise, she still has the same purple walls and gigantic bed that fits the two of us. I plop down on her bed and fiddle with the remote. The selection screen for *Love, Simon* stares back at me. Naomi appears a few seconds later with a bowl of popcorn and two Capri Sun packets.

"Okay," she says, getting herself settled. "You can start now."

I hit play and Naomi passes the popcorn.

Technically, we should be doing our homework, but it's April of junior year. We both need a break. We've seen *Love, Simon* before, but it's kind of the perfect *I'm all schooled out* movie. Except I can't stop thinking about Siobhan. And girls in general. Especially because the girl who plays Leah is really cute.

"Do you remember Bible Camp Isabel?" I ask, leaning against Naomi's shoulder. She glances up from the screen, unimpressed.

"The one you kissed?"

"Yeah," I say. "I wonder if she was gay or if she just hated God."

Naomi and I used to go to Bible camp every summer at our church, back when I was really into God. Isabel didn't care about doing crafts or memorizing Bible verses. I thought she was weird. But she wasn't afraid to kiss a girl on the lips during Truth or Dare, and neither was I.

"Why can't it be both?" Naomi gives me a suspicious look. "And what's with all the weird questions about church camp? Be quiet and watch the movie."

Simon is dressed up like a hippie or Jesus or something.

"I'm just thinking about girls," I say, leaning back so I can see Naomi's face. "And the first time I kissed one."

I still remember it, even though I was ten then. Her lips were soft and sweet from the Teddy Grahams we ate for a snack. I remember it lasted for a few seconds and nothing more. Afterward, everyone stared at us with wide eyes, like we'd just slayed a dragon or something. The year after that, Isabel wasn't at Bible camp. I got bored of singing songs and making lanyards. Naomi and I stopped going when we were twelve.

"Hmmm." Naomi gives me a knowing look. "Are you thinking about all girls? Or *one* in particular?"

Siobhan reminds me of Isabel, but I don't know why. I can barely conjure up Isabel's face anymore. I just think of tan skin and warm lips. Those are things I associate with Siobhan, too, even though I have no idea what her lips feel like. I wish I did. But the chances of finding out seem pretty slim.

"Well," I say. "Actually, I wanted to talk to you about—"

"Wait," Naomi says, holding up a hand. "I really like this part."

"It doesn't seem fair that gay people have to come out," Simon says on-screen. *"Why should straight be the default?"*

I can't even blame Naomi for cutting me off. Honestly, it's one of my favorite parts of the movie. Why *should* straight be the default? I haven't told my mom that I like girls, and I kind of wish I didn't have to. I wish no one assumed that I'm straight.

"He's right, you know," Naomi says.

I roll my eyes and shove her shoulder. She laughs. This close to her, I can see she's wearing new earrings, ones with her name spelled out in gold. I know she got them for her birthday because she talked about it at lunch.

"Honestly." I lean back against her headboard. "I just feel like coming out shouldn't be this dramatic, sad thing. No one should be crying about it. You should be able to make it however you want. People should be happy to announce that they're queer."

"I think more people would be happy to come out if the world didn't suck," Naomi says.

"You don't even have to be happy," I say. It's hard to decide what I'm trying to say. "I wish you could figure it out when you want to and tell who you want and share it how you want. You know? But there are so many expectations and assumptions."

Naomi nods thoughtfully.

"Society forces you to do it."

"Yeah."

"What if . . ." Naomi cocks her head. "What if you did it on your own terms?"

If I had the option, I would choose not to have to come out at all. But since I don't . . .

"My terms would be, like, a big celebration," I say. "A party."

This actually sounds really good. I picture my own coming-out party, wearing a rainbow dress, walking out into a ballroom while rainbow confetti is shot out of a cannon somewhere with Tegan and Sara playing in the background. Being the center of attention. My sexuality being celebrated instead of shunted to the side where I can only talk about it with Naomi.

"Wait," Naomi says, sitting straight up. "Mahalia. That's kind of fucking genius."

"I could have it at the same place you had your party," I say, counting on my fingers. "With, like, catering and stuff, like a Sweet Sixteen, only not."

"I can ask my parents how much it was," Naomi says, pausing the TV. "Like right now."

I scrunch up my lips. Talking about money is something I do with Mom all the time, mostly when she's telling me we can't afford anything, but it feels weird for Naomi to ask her parents. But before I can say anything, Naomi has whipped out her phone and her hands are flying over the keys.

"Okay," Naomi says. "Dad said he's not telling me because it was a gift. Mom says the restaurant was two hundred dollars per hour and sixty-five dollars per plate."

My eyes widen. That's . . . a *lot* of money.

My brain switches into overdrive, trying to map this out. I could just invite Naomi and her family. Mom. A few classmates I talk with more than others. Maybe even Siobhan, if she doesn't think it's too weird. That small of a party shouldn't cost too much.

"You should do it," Naomi says, offering me the popcorn bowl. "Really. I'll help you plan."

"Really?"

"Of course," Naomi says. "I wanna go to this party."

Thinking about the price tag is kind of terrifying, honestly. But with my after-school job . . . maybe I could swing it? If I saved up?

"Yeah," I say. Excitement jumps around in my belly. "Me too."

"So you're gonna do it?"

"Yeah." I grin. "I'm gonna do it."

Naomi lets out a whoop and claps her hands together. I can't help but laugh.

We're really gonna do this. I'm really gonna have a party celebrating how gay I am.

And I can't wait.

* * *

It turns out budgeting a party is a lot more work when you don't have much money to begin with.

As soon as I get home, I start plugging away at numbers, and instantly come out with a ridiculous sum: $3,713.40 to rent the same venue as Naomi and hire their in-house caterer. When the number comes up on my calculator, I blink more times than I thought possible.

That much money for a *party*? I want to go all out, but I can't even wrap my mind around spending that much, even if it's supposed to be one of the best days of my short life.

So I go back to the drawing board. By the time Mom stumbles through the door at 7:30, I have a budget that seems more reasonable.

MAHALIA'S COMING-OUT

Number of guests: 20?

Party duration: 3 hours

REFRESHMENTS

Rainbow cake: $70, 10-inch cake

Catering: $27 per person, so $540 in total

DECORATIONS AND VENUE

Napkins, plates, etc.: $38

Venue rental: about $500

Chocolate favors: $10

ENTERTAINMENT

DJ: $250

TOTAL: $1,408

That final price is still a big number, but not nearly as big as the first one I came up with. I slump back in my seat at the kitchen table with a satisfied grin.

"Well, well, well," Mom says, kicking off her shoes. "I hope that grin on your face means you got your homework done."

"Sort of," I say, which isn't a lie, since I did some at Naomi's house. "But I have something even more exciting to show you."

Mom pulls out the seat opposite me, making a "hmph" sound. Instead of asking what I want to show her, she says, "How is Naomi doing?"

"She's fine." I wave my hand. "Actually, we were talking about her party. That's what I—"

She sighs, almost soft enough that I don't hear, eyes shutting. Mom looks dead whenever her eyes close. It freaks me out.

"Mahalia," she says. "We already talked about this—"

"I know," I say before she can make her speech about how we're poor and we can't afford anything and we would be getting food stamps if we didn't make slightly too much to qualify. "But we were talking about it and I was thinking I could have a delayed party."

It's not *technically* a lie. A coming-out party is a delayed party. Mom just doesn't need to know about the whole *coming-out* part. I'll tell her during the party, or maybe she won't understand what's really going on. I don't know. If she lets me do it, I'll figure that stuff out later.

She hums but doesn't say anything. It's her way of saying she'll think about it. I can't tell if she's leaning toward yes or no, but if I'm paying for it, do I actually need her permission?

"Where are you going to get the money for that?"

"I'm going to save," I say, pushing my budget toward her. "I know this is a lot. Don't freak out. But look."

I point to the calculations at the bottom. I make $360 every two weeks at my part-time job, so if I use what's already in my bank account and work to save up the rest, I could probably have the party in a little under two months. It all seems so possible.

Mom raises a brow as she reads. I can't tell if she's impressed or not.

"Hmm," she says. "What if I matched what you managed to save?"

Her expression betrays nothing, but Mom isn't the type to toy with me like this. Not unless I'm in trouble. I don't think I am right now.

"Would you really?"

I can't keep the excitement out of my voice. If Mom paid for half—I could be looking at a coming-out party in a month.

"I can't make any promises," she says. "But I'll try my best."

I grin, practically launching myself at her.

"All right, all right," she says, pulling me in for a hug. "No guarantees, okay? And make sure you have enough for gas and your phone bill."

But I'm not listening to her, not really. I'm going to have my fucking party. How can I focus on bills at a time like this?

"I have to call Naomi," I say, grabbing my phone. "Thank you, thank you, thank you!"

Mom grins tiredly at me. Then I'm rushing down the hallway and dialing Naomi's number.

CHAPTER 5

There's a problem on Tuesday. I'm sitting in a group with Danny, textbooks open, and Siobhan isn't here.

In her defense, class only started ten minutes ago, but it's long past the bell. Enough time for everyone to get into their groups and start chattering like we're in the cafeteria. Everyone except Danny and me, anyway. It would be an awkward silence—if Danny weren't banging on the desk with his sticks, nodding like he's deep in the groove, backing up Maroon 5 or something.

"So," I say, raising my voice. "What do you think about the Great Recession?"

"Too recent." Danny wrinkles his nose. "Doesn't really count as *history,* you know?"

I bite my lip so my frown isn't too obvious. Isn't *anything* that happened in the past history?

"Okay," I say, flipping a page in my textbook. "So that counts out Obama's presidency, right?"

Danny hits the desk particularly hard and I jump.

"*What if,*" he says, "we did the 2000 election?"

"That's not too recent for you?"

"I mean," Danny says, scratching the back of his head with a stick. "We weren't born yet."

He's got me there.

"Okay," I say, jotting down notes. "So the 2000 election. The controversy over the popular vote and—*oh,* you know what would be cool? We can connect this back to the lesson on the creation of the electoral college and how it has to do with slavery and Bush during Hurricane Katrina—"

"Whoa, whoa, whoa," Danny says. His drumming has stopped. "I don't know about all that. We probably shouldn't get political. We can just—"

"I mean," I say. "History is political."

It's something Mr. Willis said during the first week of class. I remember because it surprised me—none of my other teachers have admitted that *any* of our subjects can be political.

"Well," Danny says. "Maybe we can just leave that part out."

"How, though?" I say. "It's literally an election. Even if you don't want to talk about it, different historical events impact each other, and Bush's presidency definitely impacts—"

The door swings open. It's Siobhan, in all her messy-haired glory, holding a clear Starbucks cup and wearing a pair of overalls that look like she grabbed them from her bedroom floor. Not that I'm judging—that's how I figure out my outfits most mornings. But I can't help being excited that we have something in common. Then I want to smack myself for being so geeked out over something so small.

Siobhan looks over at us first, flashing a small, tired smile. I wave back at her like a nerd. It takes me a long moment to realize she's actually looking at Danny, her *boyfriend.*

I'm an idiot.

Siobhan makes it halfway across the room before Mr. Willis clears his throat. A few people look up, stop their conversations.

"I'm sorry," she says, digging into her pocket, placing a late slip on his desk. "I got to school early this morning, but then the coffee line was so long and I've just been running late all day."

She slurps a little too loudly. I wince. If there's one thing this man hates, it's food or drinks in class, and the combination of Siobhan showing up late *with* Starbucks is practically making his eye twitch out of its socket.

"Miss Davidson," he says, voice tight. "Perhaps you aren't aware, but we have a no-drinks rule in this class."

Danny starts with the drumsticks again, hitting them against the desk quickly, almost like he's trying to kill a bug. I kick at his leg.

"Ow," he yelps. "What was that—"

I cough loudly and turn back to Mr. Willis, who is staring at Siobhan like *she's* the bug.

"There's only a bit left," she says. "Could I just finish—"

"It's policy," he says. "Technically against school rules to have any food in classrooms."

"It's just . . ." She swallows, lowering her voice. "I missed breakfast this morning and—"

"I'm sorry, Miss Davidson," Mr. Willis says, holding the garbage can out toward her. "Rules are rules."

Siobhan actually looks my way. At first, I think she's looking at Danny, like she was before. But then her eyes narrow, and I realize I'm actually the one she's focused on. But why is she looking at *me*? Does she expect me to do something? If Mr. Willis won't listen to her, he won't listen to me.

With a sigh, Siobhan tosses the cup in the garbage can. And for the rest of class, she barely talks—or makes eye contact with me again.

* * *

"So she looked at you like she wanted help?"

"That's what it felt like," I say. "But I don't know what I was supposed to do. It's not like Willis would listen to me, you know?"

Naomi glances up, unimpressed. Her Fresh Abundance smock is free of wrinkles and actually looks good on her. It's completely unfair. She turned sixteen a few days ago and she's already better at it than me.

"Maybe it's not about that," she says. "Maybe she just wanted some support."

"Support?" I sigh heavily. "Danny was literally right there."

"That doesn't mean you couldn't do anything." Naomi glances behind me. "Aren't you supposed to be on register right now?"

Fresh Abundance is a small natural foods store. Since it's independently owned and not a chain, we only have four registers. Technically, three of us are supposed to be on them. Naomi is at hers. I'm not at mine. Bill, this old dude who should be retired but works here to get out of the house, is at his station, chatting happily with another old person. Without Naomi and Bill, I'm pretty sure this place would crash to the ground.

"You and Bill look like you're doing fine," I say, waving a hand. "Anyway, this is important."

"I already told you what to do," Naomi says. "Be more supportive."

I open my mouth to respond, but she scoffs like she's already irritated by whatever I might say.

"What about the party," she says. "How is the planning going?"

Normally I'd be irritated at the subject change, but the party is the only other thing I'm excited about. I pull a little pad out of my pocket and fan the pages.

"I've been writing stuff in this little notebook," I say. "We have a budget. We have a cake—rainbow, of course. My mom's on board."

"All excellent." Naomi grins. "What type of music are you gonna play?"

"Gay music," I say before I even think. She shoots me a glare. "Uh, okay. I'm trying to think of gay songs. Maybe 'Same Love' by—"

"Mahalia, I swear to *God*—"

"Okay, okay," I say. I crack myself up.

"Maybe . . . wait, wait, wait!" She claps her hands. "You know that Diana Ross song that they played in *Maid in Manhattan*? When J.Lo was getting her makeover done before she went to see that rich white guy at the fancy dance?"

"I hate you," I say. "That's 'I'm Coming Out' and it's a fucking classic and I'm disappointed you don't know it."

"I know it, I just couldn't remember the name. And you're always disappointed about my music tastes."

This is true, but it feels rude to say out loud.

"And I guess Hayley Kiyoko," Naomi continues, gesturing toward my notebook. "Even though that might be *too* gay."

I snatch a pen from her register and start scrawling all the names.

"Nah," I say. "Hayley is never too gay. But I think I'll walk out to 'I'm Coming Out.' It'll be super dramatic and classy."

"Okay," Naomi says. "Not to be the boring one, but have you figured out how to pay for it?"

"I already told you." I feel a flash of irritation. "My mom's on board. She's going to pay half."

"And you're going to pay the rest?"

I don't like how disbelieving she sounds.

"Yeah," I say, shoving my notebook back in my pocket. "I already have two hundred saved. I only need five hundred more. That's, like, a month's pay."

"Ok*ay*," Naomi says. "But I just—you know I could help, right? You don't have to do it on your own."

God. This is even worse than her judgment. I shake my head.

"I'm not taking money from you."

"Mahalia, stop it. I've told you it's not a big deal—"

"Yeah, that's the problem," I say, shoving my hands in my apron pockets. "Money's not a big deal for you and it is for me. Okay? So I'm not taking it from you."

She's silent.

It's bad enough that she gave me five hundred dollars for my birthday in February. I tried to give it back and she actually got mad at me. Money has never been this big of a deal in our friendship before. The older we get, the harder it is to avoid.

"I think I can do this, Naomi," I say, staring down at her station. "I really do."

"That's good," she says after a moment. "That's really good."

I make minimum wage. Most of my paycheck goes to gas and my cell phone—which Mom refuses to pay for—and my nonexistent college fund. But I could make it work for a month.

"I really want to do this, Naomi," I say, my voice soft. "It sounds like so much fucking fun."

I've never heard of anyone doing something like this. I could get the whole *coming-out* part out of the way without having to tell a million people individually, or worse—posting a corny picture of myself on Instagram, announcing that I'm "out and proud," and all my acquaintances ignoring it.

"I want a big dress, too," I say in a rush, looking at my sneakers. "Like, a big ball gown. A pink one."

"Not a rainbow one?"

I glance up. She's grinning. Not making fun. God, I love her.

"We'll find you one," she says, squeezing my arm. "Do you have a guest list yet?"

I'm just about to answer when Greta comes flowing over to us.

"Girls! It's so lovely to see the two of you."

I have to resist the urge to roll my eyes every time I see my boss. She's this white lady with "locs," meaning she hasn't washed her hair in at least a year. I frown every time I see her head.

"How is the sun treating you today?" she asks. "I like to think of sunny days like this as something of a gift. Today is supposed to be a time for all of us to give thanks and be at one with the Earth, don't you think so?"

I glance at Naomi out of the corner of my eye. Somehow, she manages to keep a straight face.

"Oh, most definitely," I say, stepping away from Naomi. "I feel the sun in my very bones, right this instant."

Naomi nudges me in the side, but Greta nods solemnly, like I've just said something important.

"You're an Aries, aren't you, Naomi?" Greta says. "I have the sense that today is a great day for you to try something new. And, Mahalia . . ."

I frown. I've been working here for two months and have managed to keep my star sign a secret. No way I'm giving it up now.

"Her birthday's in February," Naomi supplies, ignoring my glare. "The fifteenth."

"Ah." Greta clasps her hands together. "An Aquarius! I think you should commit to more of a team spirit this month, Mahalia. You could use the help of others."

"Um." I blink. "Okay."

"If you give me a moment, I can go back in my office and give you a more accurate—"

"Oh, look!" I say, pointing at a dude who moves toward my lane. "It looks like I have to get back to work. Talk to you soon, Greta!"

Naomi is probably going to kill me for leaving her alone with Greta. I just can't do it. The longer I'm around our boss, the more likely I am to get both of us fired. Well, Naomi is a great employee and everyone loves her. I'm the only one who'd get fired—and I'm the one who actually needs this job. Naomi just wants to put this on college applications.

The man in my lane is wearing a suit and keeps looking down at his phone. I recognize him before I get to the register. He comes in once a week to buy pretentious-looking shit like organic kale. And he's kind of hot. He has blond hair and blue eyes—very California surfer type, but the suit doesn't go with the vibe.

"Hi! How are you?" I ask. "Did you find everything all right?"

He grunts. I slide the kale into his reusable bag and give him his change.

"Have a *wholesome* day," I say between gritted teeth. He barely nods before picking up the bags and walking toward the door. It jingles when it shuts behind him. I roll my eyes. Bill glances at me, gives a shrug like he's saying, "What are you gonna do?"

"Mahalia, I *hate* you," Naomi hisses, appearing next to me. "Next time you leave me alone with her, I'm gonna make sure you end up locked in her office when she's doing astrology charts for the month."

"Come on," I say, leaning an arm against her shoulder. "You know I would've started laughing. You have a better poker face."

"You just wanted to see Kale Guy."

"Not really," I say, and it's only half a lie. "You know he never pays attention to me, anyway. I'd rather be with you."

She narrows her eyes. I smile.

I've known Naomi since I was ten and we were at the beginning of sixth grade. Before then, I really didn't talk during school, but Naomi was having her period and my mom had already taught me about mine, so I gave her my sweatshirt and told her what to do in the bathroom. We've been like sisters ever since then and almost look like it, because of our dark skin and eyes. Naomi's eyes are narrower and her mouth is bigger. She also wears her hair in box braids, unlike me, whose curls have never met a hair tie they can't break.

"Okay," I say. "But for real. What am I supposed to do about Danny?"

"I thought we were talking about Kale-Chip Guy?"

"No, I need you to be my life coach again." I shake my head. "What do I do?"

"There's nothing for you to do?" Naomi says it like it's a question. "You can have a crush on her, but that's her boyfriend. Don't be weird."

I groan.

"Come on," Naomi says. "He's not so bad."

"You're only saying that because you like him."

"Not anymore," she says, nudging my shoulder. "Not like *that*. Not since Cody. And everyone's had a crush on him. I'm not the only one. You can't just hate every white rich guy, you know."

"I don't *hate* him," I say, even though I'm not sure whether it's true or not. "And anyway, if I did, it wouldn't be because of that. It'd be because he's a cardboard cutout of every other popular guy in existence. He only has a 4.0 GPA because his parents have the money to hire tutors. They bought him a car. He can basically buy whatever he wants."

"That's . . ." Naomi frowns. "My parents would find me a tutor, too, if I needed. Does that make me a bad person?"

"God," I say, tossing my head back. "Of course not, Naomi. I'm just . . ."

I don't know what I mean. Danny lives in the same neighborhood as Naomi. They both have parents who make a lot of money. But somehow, Naomi manages not to be nearly as insufferable as him. I don't know why. Maybe because she's Black. Maybe because she's interesting and cool and kind and doesn't bring drumsticks to class. Maybe because she's just Naomi and there isn't a specific reason, but a million.

"I just said the wrong thing," I say, bumping my hip with hers. "Come on. Don't be mad."

"Okay," she says. "Sure."

I can't tell if she's convinced or not.

CHAPTER 6

Naomi and I have the same English class but sit across the room from each other. Usually we spend the period trying to catch each other's eye and make goofy faces, depending on what our teacher, Mr. Lewis, is talking about. More often than not, when we're talking about race.

But on Wednesday, instead of listening to our white classmates eagerly volunteer to read aloud from *Huckleberry Finn* so they can say the word *nigger,* I'm staring at Danny—whose hand is raised higher than anyone else's.

"Danny," Mr. Lewis says. "Next page, please."

Danny actually clears his throat. I make eye contact with Naomi across the room and mime sticking my finger down my throat. She tosses her head back dramatically and holds a hand over her heart, like she's just been stabbed.

"'Oh, yes, this is a wonderful govment, wonderful,'" Danny reads aloud in an exaggerated Southern drawl. "'Why, looky here. There was a free nigger there from Ohio—'" And when he says the word, it's like he can barely hide his excitement. "'A mulatter, most as white as a white man. He had the whitest shirt on you ever see, too, and . . .' "

I know I shouldn't judge him more than I judge the other kids—at least half of the class has volunteered to read so far and there's always this sick sense of glee when they do, like they're getting away with something. But Danny seems to relish it more than most.

I hate this.

I'm not the type of person who gets upset when I hear rappers use the n-word in songs or when it shows up on TV, but that's usually because they're Black. I've always felt like we all have different connections to the word, to the history of it, and we all have to decide for ourselves how to face it moving forward. It doesn't feel like something one Black person can decide for another. But the fact that my mom never says it, that I've seen Black students like Marcus, Naomi's brother, get in trouble for saying it, but Mr. Lewis doesn't have anything to say about non-Black kids reading it out loud in class? That he's not even going to moderate, to have a talk with us about why this is weird? We're just going to chalk it all up to the time and history? It makes my stomach twist.

" 'They call that a govment that can't sell a free nigger till he's been in the State six months. Here's a govment that calls itself—' "

"Thank you, Danny," Mr. Lewis says. "Next volunteer?"

I know Naomi is trying to make eye contact with me, but I can't take my eyes off Danny. Off the way he smirks and giggles whenever his friends read the word, right until the bell rings for lunch. *This* is the guy Siobhan is with? I can't tell if what I feel is judgment or pity.

Our school has an open campus, which means you're allowed to leave for lunch once you're a junior. It's probably the only good thing about this year full of trying to maintain a decent GPA and stressing about the SAT—if I ignore the fact that it's one of the biggest drains on my bank account. Today, instead of dropping by the local deli or hitting up a fast-food place, I head to the Starbucks drive-thru.

"Can you believe that?"

"I feel like I shouldn't be surprised," I say, pulling up behind the fifth person in line. "But I still am. Like, are we supposed to just be okay with that?"

"I thought he'd talk about how important language was," Naomi says. "When Marcus had to read *Huck Finn,* he said his teacher told them she wanted the n-word said out loud so that they could understand how ugly the language was."

"Ugh." I gag. "Wouldn't we already know?"

"Of course." Naomi smacks her hands against her thighs. "The worst part is—I just want all my teachers to like me, you know?"

"Oh yeah." I pull up a little. "I definitely know."

Naomi's the type of kid every teacher likes. When we were little, it was because she barely spoke in class. And when she speaks up now, she always seems to know exactly what they want to hear.

"But it's so weird with Mr. Lewis," she says. "He does stuff like that in class, and I *still* want him to like me, you know? And I don't know how to say something and be polite, so I just don't say anything at all. The whole thing makes me hate him a little."

I kind of get where she's coming from. Even though I don't

care much about whether or not a teacher likes me, there's still something extremely stressful about criticizing the way someone talks about race—*especially* if it's an adult.

But Naomi knows all that, so instead, I grin at her and say, "Only a little?"

She elbows me. Before I can defend myself, it's our turn to order.

I'm not really a coffee girl. I don't know all the special flavors and additives. The menu is big enough, but I know people personalize the hell out of their drinks, and I'm not even sure where to start. Maybe this wasn't the best idea after all.

But I'm at the front of the line, and the speaker is chirping, "Welcome to Starbucks, what can I get you?" And then it's too late to turn back around.

"Um," I say. "Do you have a coffee that's, like, milky?"

There's a pause. Naomi slaps her forehead. I actually hate myself.

"Do you mean a regular coffee with milk?" the voice asks. "Or maybe a latte?"

"A latte sounds good," I say. "One with ice?"

I *think* that's what Siobhan brought to class yesterday.

"And which one would you like?" the voice chirps. "The Starbucks Reserve? Iced Cinnamon Dolce? Blonde Vanilla? Hazelnut Bianco—"

"Um, I think the . . . regular one?" I clear my throat and glance at Naomi, who just shrugs. "Whichever normal one you have."

Another pause. I wonder if this person is confused as hell, or just irritated. I've had my fair share of weirdos at Greta's and now

I've become one. I'm about five seconds from hopping the curb out of the drive-thru and never coming anywhere near this shopping center for the next fifteen years.

"Okay." The voice sounds almost resigned. "That'll be $5.75."

"Jesus," Naomi breathes out. "That was painful. And this is all for Siobhan?"

"Well," I say, trying my best not to sound defensive. "Yeah."

When I described Siobhan to Naomi, she instantly recognized her—Naomi's mom and Siobhan's dad studied abroad together, apparently. Even though I peppered Naomi with questions about her, Naomi didn't seem to know much, which leaves me doing things like . . . *this* to win Siobhan over.

By the time I get back to school, my lunch period is almost over, and I head straight to Mr. Willis's room with hope high in my chest. The plan is to catch Siobhan early and give the drink to her before class officially starts. I'm trying not to think about what'll happen if she shows up late again. Mr. Willis might make me throw it out before she even sees it—my $5.75 gone down the drain. But I think it could be worth it.

Maybe.

I make it to the room and peek my head inside. Willis isn't sitting at his desk, which means he's probably coming back from the teachers' lounge or maybe his own lunch period. Great. My eyes flicker over to our desks. Siobhan's is empty, but Danny is already at his. Fuck. My heart sinks to the pit of my stomach. I'm turning to toss the coffee in a trash can when someone bumps into me.

"Oof," Siobhan says. "I'm sorry."

She smiles at me. I stare at her like a weirdo for a long moment. Today her hair is pulled back in a pink scarf and a big part of me is itching to touch it. God, what is wrong with me? I shove the drink into her chest before I lose my nerve. Not that I actually touch her *chest*. That would be so weird.

Siobhan grabs the cup; her hand grasps mine. I almost drop the cup.

"For me?" Her eyes flicker up, making contact with mine, and it's hard to breathe for a second. "Mahalia, this is so nice of you, but I only drink Blonde Vanilla lattes."

I blink. My mouth parts, but nothing comes out.

"I'm kidding." There's a mischievous twinkle in her eye. "Completely, absolutely kidding. This is one of the nicest things anyone has done for me since I moved here."

"Oh, it's just coffee," I say.

She takes a sip and shakes her head.

"It's not just coffee," she says. "I don't know if it's because of the time change, but I haven't been able to feel fully awake a single day since I got here. And you can imagine how that impacts the sleep schedule."

"I'm always up at night," I say. "I can't help it. I'm just used to suffering, though."

She snorts, then offers the cup to me.

"Want to try a sip?"

It's not a big deal. She's literally just offering me some of the coffee I bought her. But as I lean down and take a sip, I can't help but feel my lips tingle, like I'm doing something special. My lips touched the same straw that hers did—that seems to connect us somehow. I glance up at her, my lips around her straw, and she doesn't look like she's laughing at me. She looks like . . . she's studying me.

"All right, class." Mr. Willis comes striding into the room. "Break into your groups."

Siobhan pulls the straw away.

"Siobhan," Mr. Willis says, raising a brow. "You know the—"

"I was just about to throw it out now."

He glances between the two of us.

"Well," he says. "To your seats, ladies."

I don't even feel annoyed that Siobhan barely drank half of the coffee I got her. As we're walking across the room to our seats, she grabs my wrist, stilling me.

"Hey," she says. "We should hang out this weekend."

I literally stop breathing like I'm in *Twilight* or something.

"Yeah," I say. My voice is high-pitched as hell. "Sure. We should do that."

She smiles, her eyes crinkling, before going back to her desk, where she pecks Danny hello. He's "playing" the desk again, but instead of being annoyed like the rest of the population, Siobhan runs a hand through his hair and says, "Wow, that's really coming along."

And she sounds like she actually *means* it.

I force my eyes closed. I seriously need to chill. Even if I question her choice in men, I should respect the fact that she's with someone else.

Still. I'm allowed to have a crush. I *know* this isn't Siobhan asking me on a date. But why can't I stop the way my stomach is fluttering?

-$20 for gas
GOAL: $704

CHAPTER 7

Our car is in the parking lot when I walk home from the bus stop, which means Mom hasn't headed to work yet. It's kind of weird. Her shifts change every week, but I've gotten used to her being gone when I'm home.

"Mom," I say, walking inside the apartment. "Can I use the car?"

"No."

"But I wanna hang out with Naomi."

"Well, I need to get to work."

It was kind of stupid for me to ask—I can clearly see that she's in her scrubs and ready to go. But she takes pity on me, and that's how I end up dropping her at work so I can take the car after. Only, once I'm in the driver's seat with her next to me, I regret the entire thing.

"Lord Jesus, Mahalia, watch the swerving," Mom says, gripping her bag with both hands. "Just stay straight."

"That's kind of impossible for me." I wince once the words leave my lips. That'd be a funny joke for Naomi, but this is Mom.

"I mean. I'm not sure how," I rush on. "Not that I don't know how to keep the wheel straight. I just. Am. You know, like, a little—"

"What?" Mom asks, oblivious. "Baby, don't look at the wheel. Keep your eyes on the road. It'll help."

I guess most kids don't feel completely comfortable around their parents, but at one point, I used to tell my mother everything. We'd pray together and talk about what confused us about God and life. But that was before I started kissing girls. Even though I've caught her before a shift, I don't think now is the time to bring it up.

I move my hand toward the radio and she smacks it away. "Mom, most kids get to listen to the radio," I insist.

"I don't care what other kids are doing," she says, almost like she's reciting a speech. "You're my kid, aren't you? And try to avoid the potholes. You're hurting my fibroids."

"Is that even possible?"

"I think so," she says. "The doctor says one is as big as a twenty-eight-week fetus."

I grimace. Definitely did *not* need to know that.

"Oh, come on," she says, catching my expression. "You aren't excited about little Junior? Don't you want to say hi to your baby brother?"

She starts rubbing her stomach.

"Mom, come on." I groan. "This is *so* weird."

She giggles and I roll my eyes. After a few seconds, she relents and turns on the Christian hip-hop.

"I've been thinking," Mom says, raising her voice to be heard above the music. "We should start looking at venues soon. We'll have to put down a deposit."

A smile tugs at my lips. I can't help the slight squeal in my voice when I say, "Really?"

Mom's the sort of parent who is pretty hands-off, mostly because she works so much. But the two of us going to look at venues together, spending the day talking about the party, it all sounds like what I'd imagined when I first dreamed of having a Sweet Sixteen. I grin at her.

"Really," she says, motioning me to pull over. The nursing home is on our right. "I'll ask Maria about the schedule and find a time when we can take the afternoon, okay?"

"Okay," I say, my voice higher than usual. "I'll make a list."

She smiles at me for a moment. Then her expression goes suddenly serious.

"Now, if you get into a car accident," she says, pointing a finger at me, "we won't be able to visit anything except the hospital."

"Was that a threat?" I gasp dramatically.

"You'd better believe it," she says, but she's rolling her eyes playfully. "I'll see you later tonight."

Waving as I pull away from the curb, I head back to school and pick up Naomi, whose car is in the shop. She stayed late for student council or Key Club or one of the clubs she's always doing. I should probably get in on one of those, if only for college applications. I'm about to ask her about it when she whips out her phone.

"So," she says. "I found this website that sells really cute dresses, and they're not too expensive."

"Okay, wait." I try my best not to stare at her phone as I pull back onto the road. "What do you mean by *not expensive*? Be very clear, Naomi Lynn Sanders!"

"I mean, most of these are name-brand designers," she says,

tapping away at her screen. "But the dresses sell for only four or five hundred dollars. It's honestly a steal."

That's a steal to Naomi, but it's more than one paycheck for me. I swallow the thought down. It wouldn't hurt just to look, right?

"Okay, we'll look at the dresses," I say, "but first I want to play this record for you back at my house."

"Don't you have a portable record player?" she asks. The windows are down, like they always are, and her hair blows all over the place. "Like, isn't the point that you're supposed to bring it places?"

"I guess," I say. "But I'm not going to bring my *records* everywhere, if that's what you mean."

She scoffs as we climb out of the car and head into the apartment.

I keep my records in a gigantic pile across from my bed. Mom says it looks like a mess, but I have them organized. On the left are all the Black singers, and everyone else goes on the right. Then I organize based on name. Stevie Wonder has a pile to himself, but so do Nina Simone, Stevie Nicks, and A Tribe Called Quest. Some piles only have one or two records, like my Sade pile, but they deserve their own space nonetheless.

"Okay," I say, digging in the new record pile. "This is a Temptations record. I hope you're prepared for your limbs to be infested with funkiness."

Naomi makes a face like I just farted.

"Mahalia," she says. "You literally just ruined it."

"I didn't!"

I pull out my record player. It's already plugged in, since I like to keep it ready to play at all times, and very, *very* gingerly pull the record out of the packaging.

"You're so dramatic," Naomi says, tossing herself onto my bed. "These aren't even vintage records! You get them from Amazon!"

"Shut up," I say. "They're still extremely delicate and I don't want *any* fingerprints."

She smacks her head into my pillow. I can't hear what she mumbles, but I'm sure it's something about what a freak I am. I ignore it and place the record on the player.

My favorite part is when it starts spinning. I don't pay much attention in science classes, but I like to think of all that energy, all the soul and music and lyrics, everything that makes the record a record, and how it's pressed together in this thin black disk. It's all there. You just can't see it.

I wait for another second or two before putting the needle at the very edge.

Mom thinks it's weird that I wanted a record player so bad, but Dad understood. Before he had his new girlfriend and their own kids, he understood music, and he understood me. Sometimes it makes me feel weird, to listen to the same music I know he loves. I don't know why. It's not like he's dead, just in a different neighborhood. But still.

"Wait," I say, snapping out of my thoughts. "Naomi, you can't just pick up the needle like that!"

"Isn't that how you skip over parts?"

"Okay," I say, glaring at her. "But why are you trying to skip over the beginning of 'Papa Was a Rolling Stone'? I'm going to disown you, Naomi."

"Are you serious?" She rolls her eyes. "It's literally a twenty-minute introduction—"

"It's, like, five. Chill."

Naomi blows out a steady sigh, rolling her eyes up toward the ceiling. She puts the needle down and the song starts to play: *Duh duh. Duh duh, duh duh, duh duh.* Steady thumping and the sound of a stick hitting something. A funky guitar. I can't help but move my head to the beat.

"I can't believe I'm friends with you," she says, folding her arms. "You're such an old white guy."

I kick her leg as I climb up on my bed. We sit like that for a while: my head on her chest and her foot over mine. I know I'm the only one really listening to the album, especially when she pulls out her laptop, but it's fine. What matters the most is that I'm not alone.

Eventually, the needle makes it all the way to the center of the record. Instead of flipping it over, I take it off and start putting things away, while Naomi blasts Lorde from her laptop. I don't mind Lorde; she's pretty great. She seems cool and safe enough to offer my heart to. Because that's what picking favorite songs is, really. You offer up your heart so that the song can latch onto you. You let yourself think back to your own dad who left ("Papa Was a Rolling Stone") or your own hopes for the future ("A Change Is Gonna Come") or your thoughts of the one you love (literally a million songs have been written and produced on the subject). You can just sit back and listen to music, but you have to open yourself up, especially if someone else chose the songs for you.

"I wanna play Lorde at my party."

Naomi nods, still tapping at her computer.

"I think that's a pretty good choice. Have you figured out a date yet?"

"Not totally, but I'm thinking the end of the summer," I say. "Mom and I are planning a day to go venue touring."

"Nice." She smiles over at me. "We'll have to make a playlist for you. Maybe you can save money on a DJ that way."

"Definitely," I say, plopping up on the edge of the bed. "You know what would be cool? If I made Siobhan a mixtape."

It comes out of nowhere, but as soon as it's out of my mouth, it doesn't sound like that bad of an idea.

"What?" she says. "Like, in *The Perks of Being a Wallflower* when Charlie makes a mixtape for Sam and keeps putting that depressing song by the Smiths on it?"

"I don't think he put that on the one for Sam," I say, even though I don't remember. It's been a while since we watched the movie together. "But yeah, like that. I feel like it'd be super romantic."

Because Naomi is a good person, she doesn't roll her eyes and remind me that Siobhan has a boyfriend and I should be trying to get over her. She props her head up on her elbow instead.

"I mean," she says. "Why don't you just make her a playlist?"

"Ugh." I toss my head back and groan. "It's not the *same*."

"Well, go ahead and put the Smiths on it, then."

"I hate you."

"No, you don't." She picks her laptop back up. "I'm a genius."

* * *

After picking Mom up from work that night, I don't see the text right away.

I'm *supposed* to be going to sleep. But instead, I lay in bed and listen to entire albums on my record player, snuggling up to it like it's a pet. Tonight, it's *The Low End Theory* by A Tribe Called Quest. I'm being soothed by Phife's verses when my phone starts vibrating.

It's a text from an unknown number: *hey Mahalia. It's Siobhan. Hope it's okay to reach out! I wanted to make sure we could keep in touch about hanging out this weekend!*

I stare at it for so long that my phone goes black.

When Siobhan said we should hang out earlier, I thought it was just something she was saying to be nice. I figured I'd have to keep reminding her of my existence to actually make it happen. But no, she went out of her way to reach out to *me*.

I turn my phone back on and stare at the screen. It's just one text, but it makes me incredibly hopeful. Even if we aren't going to kiss, I'm going to see her again, and I'll take what I can get.

First Draft of a Playlist for Siobhan

(with input from Naomi)

* "Paradise" by Sade

  Wait, is this too seductive? I can't tell if putting Sade on a playlist for someone you just met is too forward or not.

  I think Sade is sort of for parents to grind to at parties and nothing else, sorry.

  I disagree but also . . . you're not completely wrong.

* "If It Isn't Love" by New Edition

* "Pictures of You" by the Cure

  This is like hella New Wave–like, but maybe she'll like it because she's European.

  It's one of the most romantic songs of all time.

  . . . okay.

* "Don't You (Forget About Me)" by Simple Minds

  This could come across as a little desperate.

  It's CLASSIC, Naomi, shut up.

  I'm just saying!!!

* "Electric Relaxation" by A Tribe Called Quest

  Isn't this the one where he talks about getting semen on her furniture?

  It was Seaman's Furniture and it was a play on words!!!

  . . . I would still rethink.

* "Just Can't Get Enough" by Depeche Mode

  ????? Like the one by the Black Eyed Peas?

  God, no, Naomi. Now we have to listen to it.

* "Walking on the Moon" by the Police

  I don't think anyone likes the Police except for you.

  SHUT UP, NAOMI!!!

* "No Diggity" by Blackstreet
  This is kind of forward.
  Is that bad?
  No . . . not necessarily.

* "I Wanna Dance with Somebody" by Whitney Houston

* "Stand by Me" by Ben E. King
  This sounds kind of like a wedding song. Isn't it a little soon to ask her to stand by you?
  But it's . . . super romantic.
  Okay, Mahalia, take this risk if you have to.

CHAPTER 8

I have to wait until Saturday to meet up with Siobhan. In between trying to study for the SAT math section and doing my homework a period before it's due, I'm whispering to Naomi about where I can find a ball gown and thinking about what Siobhan and I are going to do together, what we're going to talk about, how we're going to interact. When Saturday finally does come, I have no idea how I'm supposed to conduct myself. Especially since she picked a slightly odd place to meet up.

"Are you allowed to go to a dog park if you don't have a dog?"

"I think so?" Naomi pulls up to the entrance. "But I'm guessing Siobhan has a dog if she suggested this."

It's only 10 a.m., earlier than I'd normally wake up on a weekend, but there's already a good number of dogs—and owners—wandering around. There's a small, sandy area where dogs are let off their leashes, barking and going at each other with tongues lolling out of their mouths. It reeks of shit. Hopefully Siobhan wants to hang out in the other areas of the park—there's a big grassy meadow and it looks like there might be a trail. I swallow. This isn't a *date*, obviously.

"Naomi, help." I rub my hands against my trousers. They're already sweaty. "Am I supposed to, like, be good with this dog? Bond with this dog? Does she expect me to form a strong friendship with—"

"Jesus, Mahalia." Naomi puts the car in park. "Just be yourself. Don't worry about the romance part yet. Just focus on being friends."

"Okay, but making friends is weird. I have no idea how to make friends. I don't have any friends besides you."

"Mahalia," Naomi says, rolling her eyes. "You have tons of friends."

"Name one."

"Cal."

"Your little sibling doesn't count." Suddenly, I feel cold. "What if she thinks I'm boring?"

"You're not boring," she says, glancing pointedly out the window. "Just a little annoying."

"Thanks."

"Seriously," she says, putting a hand on my shoulder. "I doubt she's expecting this to be, like, a job interview or something. She's not going to ask you about your extracurriculars or your grades. Just be yourself and make your stupid gay jokes and everything will be fine."

"Stupid?" I frown. "I thought you loved them."

"I do." She squeezes. "Now get out of my car."

I text Siobhan to let her know I'm here, but I see her before she can respond. She's in the dog run—the sandy area that smells like shit—waving at me from a bench. Part of me wants to turn away. The scent of dog crap is *strong* and certainly not what I imagined when I thought about getting to know Siobhan. But maybe this is who she is. Maybe she's the type of person who doesn't notice the smell of dog poop. I'm not sure if that's a deal breaker or not.

At least she isn't wearing open-toed shoes. Her hair is pulled back in a little ponytail decorated with a multicolored bandanna, and she has on jeans, Blundstone boots, and a red flannel. My queer senses go off immediately. Sure, straight girls can wear flannel, but is it *really* a coincidence that Siobhan would wear a flannel the first time we hang out together? She's obviously sending me some sort of sign.

Or I'm obviously pathetic.

"Mahalia!"

Before I can even greet Siobhan, a gigantic dog comes barreling toward me. I'm sure the shriek of fear I let out makes me look absolutely pathetic. I barely have the time to consider the fact before I'm tackled to the sand—the sand where all the dogs shit and pee. Ugh.

The dog licks at my face, leaving thick lines of slobber, and I'm helpless against the attack.

"Stop, stop, stop," I say, holding my hands over my face. Out of the corner of my eye, I can see a few people glancing at me, but mostly they go about their business. I guess it's better to know ahead of time that no one will save me if one of these dogs decides to turn me into a living chew toy.

"*Doodle,*" Siobhan says, pulling the dog back. "Buddy, *stop.*"

She calls her dog *buddy.* I'm laying on the ground, it smells like shit, and I'm sure I'll have sand all over my clothes. But the fact that she calls her dog *buddy* is the cutest fucking thing I've ever heard in my life.

"I'm sorry," Siobhan says. "She's pretty young."

Doodle is looking up at me with these big eyes and panting like I'm the best person in the world. Not sure how to reconcile that with the fact that she just *tackled* me.

Siobhan holds the dog's collar with one hand and reaches the other out toward me. I wipe the sand off on my jeans before letting her pull me up, trying my best to ignore the tingle I feel at the touch. This is *definitely* not a date.

"There," Siobhan says, looking me up and down. "Better?"

I'm sure I look like a mess. I'm wearing jeans and a Tears for Fears shirt but don't look nearly as put together as she does—especially after the fall. I tug at the edge of my shirt and try my best not to cross my arms over my chest.

"Yeah," I say. "I think so. But I might have to sue your dog for emotional distress."

"Well, I suppose I can't really blame you." Siobhan laughs, looking down. "Doodle, you might have to get a job, my friend."

Doodle starts to lick at my hand and I snatch it away.

"Aw," Siobhan says, glancing back at me. "I think she likes you."

It turns out she loves me. We can barely claim a bench and take a seat without the dog trying to jump on me again.

"This isn't fair," Siobhan says, staring as I rub my hands over Doodle's fur. "We just adopted her and it's like she likes everyone else more than me. But she's actually in *love* with you."

"It's true," I say, rubbing Doodle's head. "I suppose trauma bonds people."

I'm not the type of person to kiss dogs on their mouths—

that's white people shit. But I let Doodle lick my cheek once—just *once*—because it'll probably make me look good. It's not exactly as bad as it was the first time. Siobhan's lips turn up.

"You're funny," she says. "In a weird kind of way."

"Uh." My throat goes dry. "Thank you?"

"It's okay," she says, bumping her knee with mine. "I like weird."

In one of the corners, a gigantic dog jumps onto a smaller one, and it reminds me of the fights that sometimes happen in the school cafeteria. The owners jump up from their respective benches and jog over. Doodle watches, blinks, and jogs to a different corner.

"So," I say. "What do you usually do when you come here?"

"Sometimes we walk along the trail," Siobhan says, gesturing behind us. "There's this wooded area, nice for hiking."

I make a face.

"What?" she says. "You don't like to hike?"

"No," I say. "Honestly, I avoid almost all physical activity."

Siobhan frowns a little, looking back at Doodle.

"I like hiking," she says. "Really, I love walking. I like feeling disconnected from all the madness of the world and connecting with something more . . . innate. Does that make sense?"

"I think so," I say. "Like one of those people who decides to live off the grid because modern-day life is too unbearable."

Siobhan chuckles, shaking her head. For a second, I worry I've offended her, but she wears a crooked grin when she turns to me.

"Exactly like that. That's my goal—to become infamous for

trying to live off the grid. Me, who can't function without a white-chocolate soy milk mocha from Starbucks every morning. I'm sure I'll succeed without any access to modern amenities."

Then she rolls her eyes and makes a face while gesturing toward herself, as if to say, "Can you believe this girl?" I giggle before I can stop myself. I didn't expect this—that she'd make me laugh like this. She dresses so brightly, with the bangles and the overalls, I figured she'd be more relentlessly positive. This . . . I like this, sparring back and forth with her.

"Well," I say loftily, puffing out my chest. "We all have our flaws, like—"

"Like being afraid of dogs?"

"Excuse you," I say, holding up both hands. "I am *not* afraid of dogs."

"Mahalia," Siobhan says. My name sounds musical in her mouth. "You looked absolutely *terrified* of my dog—"

"She was running toward me!" I say. *"Running,* at *full speed,* without warning!"

"—my *golden retriever,"* she continues, grinning. "Named *Snickerdoodle."*

"Some of us," I hiss, trying to hold back my laughter, "do not have much experience with animals!"

"I know, I know," Siobhan says. "It was obvious as soon as you stepped foot into the dog run."

Maybe five minutes ago, that would've felt like a dig, but now it feels like an inside joke. I scan my brain for something snarky to say back, but Siobhan continues before I can.

"Danny said it might be weird, to bring you here," she says, tugging a little at the ends of her hair. "But I still don't know many places to go in San Diego."

I try my best not to wince at the mention of Danny. The sound of his name is like off-beat drumsticks banging against my brain.

"Oh yeah," I say, hoping that I sound chill. "How did you guys meet, anyway? Weren't you only here for a little while before you started school?"

I wince as soon as the words are out of my mouth. Siobhan just grins, wiggling her eyebrows.

"Wait a second," she says. "Are you asking me about my mad skills?"

I laugh, but it sounds garbled to my ears. "Seriously, though."

"It just sort of happened." She looks like she's trying not to smile but having a hard time. "We moved here at the beginning of March for my mum's job, but I didn't know anyone. Danny was one of the kids who offered to give me a tour before I started. We both love animals and the same type of music. He told me about the animal shelter where he volunteers, and I started going with him. Then, well . . ."

Her voice trails off. She's smiling pretty hard. I have to look away.

I had no idea Danny liked animals or volunteered at a shelter. I don't know anything about him, really, just football and "drumming." Part of me wants to ask if his banging is the "music" they bond over, but I can't bring myself to. Siobhan looks *good* happy. Her smile takes up every inch of her face and her eyes get all squinty. But *God,* Danny? Really?

"What else is there to do here?" I say, turning to look at the dogs again. Doodle is rolling around with her tongue out. "Besides the hiking and dog walking and all that."

Siobhan blinks, as if startled, but rolls with it.

"Well, it *is* a dog park," she says. "So walking and hiking are going to be the top-rated attractions."

"Right." I nod, already hating myself for changing the subject the way I did. "Totally."

"But the trails are really pretty," she says, almost shy. "Nice for taking pictures."

I turn my body a little too suddenly toward her. "You like to take pictures?"

I don't know why the idea grips me so much—the image of an artsy Siobhan, traveling the country in an old van, a bandanna in her hair, taking pictures of everything. It just seems so . . . romantic. Then I shove the feeling down. We're just *talking*. We're just *hanging out.* Jesus, Mahalia, get ahold of yourself.

"Sometimes." Siobhan smiles a little. "Not as a hobby or anything serious. Just to remember things."

"Do you have a hard time remembering things?" I ask. "Normally?"

"I have the *worst* memory," Siobhan says. "In one ear and out the other. My mum is constantly bringing up stuff I only barely recall. Do you remember being little?"

"Yeah," I say. "It wasn't that long ago—and I haven't done anything interesting like move to a different continent."

"You definitely have a point." Siobhan cups her face, making a faux-modest expression like an actress accepting an Oscar. "As an international woman of intrigue, I forget that most people lack my worldly sophistication."

I snort, then hold my hand over my mouth. Siobhan snickers.

"No, it's all right," she says. "I'm being ridiculous on purpose."

"Oh, good," I say. "I thought you were being ridiculous on accident."

A dog barks loudly and I flinch a little. I don't know if I imagine it, but Siobhan seems to shift toward me, her shoulder bumping up against mine.

"Do you know," she says, "I think you're the only student in our class who isn't afraid of Mr. Willis."

"Am I?"

Mr. Willis isn't scary. He just has annoying rules and likes to force us into group projects—annoying behavior, sure, but definitely not scary.

Siobhan nods. "And yet you're still scared of dogs."

"Oh my *God*."

Siobhan laughs, snorting a little before she covers her mouth.

"Don't say anything," she orders. *"Nothing."*

"What?" I just grin at her. "What would I say?"

She shakes her head, but when she removes her hand, she's smiling underneath. That's how being with her right now makes me feel—like I'm smiling everywhere.

CHAPTER 9

My mom and I are not the type of mother and daughter to spend tons of time together. We don't tell each other everything or act like the main characters from *Gilmore Girls*. It's not really her fault—she works long hours and I'm usually at school or hanging out with Naomi. Even when we try to make plans, say we'll have dinner together or watch a movie, something always comes up. The most one-on-one time we have together is church whenever she gets the time, around once a month.

Needless to say, when Mom actually drives us to a venue on Sunday instead of to our local church, it feels a little bit like we're in an alternate universe. Like we're the type of mother and daughter who always spend time together on the weekends. Like we don't have to scrimp and save for a party. Like it's completely normal for us to go to a place like this—something out of an episode of *The Real Housewives*.

The venue is gigantic, draped in flowering vines and Spanish moss. It looks like a villa from Italy, or at least, the way they always look on TV and in movies. I don't know why I'm so blown away—after all, I was the one who chose this place. Maybe I just can't believe Mom actually drove us here without making comments about how expensive it is.

As we step out of the car, I can tell that Mom is taking in the place, too, staring a little too long at all the luxury cars in the parking lot and inspecting the architecture like she's a historian or an art critic. When we step inside, it doesn't seem like a restaurant so much as a gigantic ballroom with more space than I can ever imagine filling. I swallow around something hard in my throat.

"I didn't know it would be like this," I say. It's only half a lie. There weren't any prices listed on the website, so I figured it must be expensive, but still. "We should honestly just—"

Suddenly, a white man appears in front of us, sporting a bushy mustache and a smile that reaches his eyes in the creepiest way possible. I almost grab Mom's hand out of fear.

"You must be Mahalia," he says. His mustache covers most of his mouth, but I can tell it's curved into a maniacal grin. "And you must be Mahalia's mother. We've been waiting for you."

I turn to Mom, trying to convey my fear through my eyes, but she just smiles at this guy like he's completely normal. God. I really am alone out here.

The creepy guy's name turns out to be Willard, a name I've never heard before in my life, but he and Mom can't seem to stop talking—about what Mom does for work, how long Willard has been working here (ten years, yikes), how far we drove to get here, and a million other things I tune out before we reach the dining room.

Which. First of all, I didn't even know there was a separate dining room. There's no way I can afford any of this. Mom doesn't even seem to register that fact, though, and keeps smiling as Willard pulls out chairs for both of us at a fancy round table covered in a gold cloth and disappears, probably back to whatever pod he hatched from.

"Mom," I hiss as soon as he's out of sight. "What are you doing?"

"What do you mean?" She opens one of the red cloth booklets in front of us. "I'm making conversation."

I'm about to remind her that we can't afford this when I realize she knows. Of course she knows. For the longest time, it was Mom who had to worry about money, while I wasn't even aware of how hard she worked to make rent. But why would she want to stay? It almost feels mean, that she'd let me sit here and pretend like I can have this when we both know I can't.

Opening the red booklet just makes it worse. The first page lists a bunch of services this place provides for parties—a photographer ($995) or a photo booth ($695) or maybe a cotton-candy cart with an attendant ($350). They seem like things someone would have at a Super Sweet Sixteen. Things that, I have to admit, I would love to have.

"They just want to bleed us dry, don't they?" Mom murmurs, flipping the page. "Imagine finding the money for all this?"

My heart sinks and I don't even know why.

"Well," I say, trying my best to keep the bite out of my voice. "I told you we could leave."

"Why would we do that?" Mom asks. "Mahalia, when are we ever going to be able to do this again?"

Before I can answer, Willard reappears with a platter of food—savory tarts topped with wild-foraged chanterelles and fresh herbs, soft cheeses drizzled in locally sourced honey, seared skirt steak atop a bed of pureed parsnips and wilted greens. It doesn't look like food for a Sweet Sixteen or even a coming-out party. It looks like the type of food they'd have at a wedding. He places it down with a flourish, glancing between the two of us.

"Feel free to try any of our main dishes," he says. "Then we can discuss pricing."

Mom grabs her fork and starts to dig in, even nudging me with her shoulder, wiggling her eyebrows and making silly faces. I know this should be a fun moment for the two of us. We're at a fancy place we'd probably never be able to afford on our own. Now I get why Mom wanted to stay—but for some reason, I feel like crying.

"Why, Lady Crumbleton," Mom says in the *worst* British accent I've ever heard. "This tart is simply *divine*. I must inquire after your cook. 'Tis *so* hard to find good help these days."

She takes a dainty bite of steak and gives a small, approving nod.

"Mom," I say. "We're in public."

"And this steak, Lady Crumbleton!" Mom raises her eyebrows as far as they can go. "It's the best I've tasted in all of my years. My poor illiterate servants couldn't cook something half as excellent."

I giggle a little, despite my best efforts.

"Mom," I say. "Your poor *illiterate* servants? Where did you even get that?"

Mom sniffs a little, poking out her pinky like she's drinking tea.

"Honestly," she says. "How difficult can it be to find a scullery maid with the wits to read a recipe?"

I snort, rolling my eyes, but Mom grins and pushes my plate toward me.

"Come on," she whispers, breaking character. "Play along. Just for a bit?"

I glance at the spread. It's probably the fanciest meal I've seen in my entire life—outside the parties Naomi's parents sometimes invite me to. Even if it makes me sad, Mom is right. When is the next time we're going to get to do this again? I pick up the cloth napkin and daintily drape it on my lap. Then I raise my complimentary glass of water with my pinky held up.

"Countess Frogsworth—"

"Frogsworth?"

"Mom," I hiss. "You picked *my* name."

"Fine, fine," she says. "Countess Frogsworth it is."

We clink our glasses together, and I can't help but smile, just a little.

CHAPTER 10

On Monday, instead of being free to enjoy my lunch period, I'm stuck in the library working on this stupid history project. When Siobhan suggested studying together after school, I told her I had to work—the truth, but it didn't get me out of this little meetup the way I somehow thought it would.

Now I'm sitting at one of the wooden tables in the corner, separated from the rest of the world. Across from Danny and Siobhan. This wouldn't suck so much if it were just Siobhan. Sadly, she and Danny are making weird googly eyes at each other. I consider perhaps tossing myself out of the window, but decide to grab my books instead. Thankfully, the sound interrupts them, and Siobhan turns to face me.

"Thank God you're here," she says as I pull out my books. "Danny and I are a little lost without you."

My cheeks warm like she's complimenting me on my charm or wit, even though she's probably just desperate—I would be, too, if I had to work on a project alone with her boyfriend.

"I'm sure you're fine," I say. "Isn't it true that Europeans are more educated?"

"Exactly true," Siobhan says without missing a beat. "But I never bothered to learn about the States, out of principle, of course."

"Of course," I repeat, grinning a little. "Well, allow me to educate you on one of our greatest failures as a nation. A failure I'm sure countries like Ireland have never experienced."

"Absolutely not," Siobhan says. "Ireland would never, uh, have a scandal about an election, was it?"

"Not like us peasants over here."

"Mahalia." Siobhan snorts. "I think you're confusing the Irish and the British. We are definitely *also* peasants. Just more refined peasants, if you will."

Danny clears his throat, jostling Siobhan a little in his lap. It was so easy to forget he was there. Siobhan's wearing a bright yellow scarf over her hair and this long peasant-top-looking thing that shows a bit more of her chest than usual. I only glance a few extra seconds—I promise I'm not a creep—but I swear Danny is watching me when I look away. Now he wraps both arms around her, squeezing her a little. Drumsticks poke out of both of his hands. I can't *believe* he brought them.

"Hey, guys," he says. "Do you wanna get started before, you know, the lunch period ends?"

Siobhan laughs, but I feel my face burn as I open my notebook.

"So," I say, clearing my throat. "The 2000 election. I was thinking we could split up the presentation into three sections— Gore's side, Bush's side, and the aftermath."

"Wait a second," Danny says. "What do you mean by *sides*?"

I hold back a sigh.

"I meant, like, their sides of the story," I say, glancing down at my notes. "Or what their lawyers would've argued in front of the Supreme Court."

"That sounds a little contentious . . ."

Jesus. This time I don't bother to hide my groan.

"Danny," I say, as gently as I can. "This was an election. Our presentation is going to be political."

"The thing is . . ." Danny rubs the back of his head with his drumstick. "It doesn't need to be. That's just the way you're trying to make it. And I don't think we should bring our personal views into the project—isn't the whole point of history to be objective?"

Is he serious? The look he gives me says he is.

Maybe back in our first year of high school, you could believe teachers when they said we could be objective while talking about this stuff—*maybe.* But you can tell nothing about history is impartial just by watching the news for a few minutes or clicking around on the *Los Angeles Times* main page. I glance at Siobhan, but her expression is unreadable. My chest fills with hot air.

"Well, I'm sorry, but it's not about what *you* think," I hear myself saying. "It's literally just how things are, so maybe you can—"

"I think we should compromise," Siobhan cuts in. "We can talk about why regular Americans would've sided with Al Gore or George Bush without picking a side. All right?"

She makes a face at Danny.

"Fine," Danny says. He raps a lone drumstick against the table before the librarian glares at him from her desk, holding a finger to her lips.

Satisfied, Siobhan turns to me with a stern look, an eyebrow elegantly arched. My eyes dart down before I can stop them. I'm practically pouting before I school my features.

Maybe it's the drumsticks. Maybe it's the arm snaked around Siobhan's hip possessively. Maybe it's the way he spreads out like he owns the place. Or maybe it's the way he looked at me before, like he could tell what I was thinking—or pointedly *not* thinking—when I looked at his girlfriend.

I don't like the way Siobhan is looking at me right now, either. Like I'm being difficult.

I swear it's not on purpose.

Danny hasn't straight-out admitted his political views in class or anything. I just get a vibe that we don't see eye to eye. I wonder what Siobhan thinks.

"Look," Siobhan says. "I would love to use all of our presentation time to talk about George Bush being the absolute worst. It would honestly be the very best part of my day."

Danny looks at her out of the corner of his eye, but she keeps her gaze on me.

"But, honestly?" She cocks her head to the side. "I mostly just want to get this over with—no offense to either of you lovely people. I'd rather finish this and actually do something fun."

Danny grins and smacks a kiss on her cheek. She smiles at him, quick, before turning back to me.

"Okay, Mahalia? Let's just get through this."

I feel a soft kick under the table.

"And *then*," she says, "you can bash every politician you hate, and I will listen with my full, rapt attention. I'll even take notes."

Something about the way she says *full attention* is, like, really attractive. It almost makes me dizzy—the idea of Siobhan looking at me, smiling when I say something funny, coming up with a snarky response—how pathetic is that? Am I really turned on by the idea of Siobhan laughing at my jokes? I sound like such a straight guy.

I can't think of anything funny at the moment, so I just nod and say, "Okay."

Siobhan leans back and grins like the cat that caught the canary—or whatever that saying is. And while she opens up her textbook, I swear I see Danny giving me the evil eye.

"Okay," I say with sweat beading on my brow. "I'm Al Gore."

Except I say it about ten times louder than I meant to, like: *"I'M AL GORE!!"* And then the entire library turns to face me like I'm completely deranged. The librarian doesn't just hold her finger to her lips—she *shushes* with a stern expression. A few of the kids glance at me and giggle. Danny snorts.

I'm dying a little inside, but then Siobhan brushes her knuckles against mine and says, "Good choice."

I'm still dying, but for an entirely different reason.

I am totally falling for Siobhan.

CHAPTER 11

Tuesday is another rare day when I get the car to myself. When Mom got a ride from her friend Maria in the morning, I thought it was a little weird, but it's something she's done before, and I'm definitely not going to look a gift horse in the mouth. It means I get to drive myself to school, stop at the local deli for lunch and get the famous kettle-cooked chips I love, and don't have to wait on Naomi for a ride home. It's as perfect as a day of school can be.

My day gets even better when the last bell rings and I walk out the door and bump right into Siobhan. Thank God her arms aren't full of books or coffee or anything that could dramatically fall all over the floor. She just makes an "oof" sound before looking up at me and smiling.

"Mahalia," she says. "Are you staying after school for SAT Prep?"

I make a face and she laughs.

"No," I say. "I actually try my best to pretend I never have to take the SAT. It's going really well."

It's a half-truth. The real truth is that Mom and I couldn't afford the fee, which was supposed to be a steal for students at one hundred bucks a pop. I mostly watch Khan Academy videos on the math portion and try my best to do the quizzes when I can. I've gotten better at the actual *content,* but not at my timing. It takes a 1350 score to make the top ten percent of test-takers—something that's practically guaranteed to get me scholarships, according to my guidance counselor. But I'm not sure how high my chances of improving are. How much can you *really* do with practice tests?

"Same here," she says. "Although I'll probably have to start studying sooner rather than later. My dad thought it would be a good idea to take the test in May, just for practice."

The May test is just two weeks away. It seems like neither of us can get away with just deciding not to think about it.

"Ew." I wrinkle my nose. "I mean, I get it. I took the PSAT last year and got a 1260, which isn't so bad. But I don't know how many times you need to practice taking a test in a big empty room under tons of pressure."

"Exactly," she says, shaking her head. "I don't even know if I want to go to college. I might like to travel after I graduate. But Dad won't hear of that—he says I still need options, something to fall back on."

I know I'm staring at her like she's a cartoon character, but I can't imagine not going to college. Neither of my parents went. Dad seems to be doing pretty well for himself, but I see the way Mom struggles, the way she scrimps and saves just so we can have what we do. College is supposed to keep that from happening—at least that's what everyone says. It feels like an obligation.

"You're not scared?" I blurt out.

"Scared?"

"I don't know," I say. "Of, like, not being able to get a job? Of debt?"

"I think I'll be in debt if I go to college, too," she says, the corner of her mouth turning up. "But I don't know. I'm not even eighteen. I don't have to have everything figured out."

I just blink at her.

"You think I'm irresponsible," she says.

"No," I say. "I'm just . . . kind of jealous."

She knocks her shoulder with mine. I try to ignore the warmth that lingers after she pulls away.

"Don't be," she says. "You could always come with me. We could teach English in other countries. Or maybe volunteer somewhere. We could hike all the major mountain ranges of the world."

I try to picture Siobhan and me in Europe. Staying in dingy motels—or hostels, whatever they're called—and visiting all the museums. Sharing pastries because we can't afford anything else. Taking the train across the continent. Visiting countries I never think about Black people going to, like Japan or South Korea. Hiking maybe ten minutes before having to turn around and go back into an air-conditioned room. It sounds . . .

I shake my head. "It sounds like a dream."

Her smile falls a little. I'm not sure if I've said the wrong thing. The school buses are pulling out of the parking lot now, along with other people's cars. Everyone is leaving. Before I can say bye, Siobhan cuts me off.

"Are you waiting for a ride, too?"

I shake my head, pulling the keys out of my pocket and waving them around.

"Nope," I say. "Just figuring out how I can get out of my college plans and go on a tour of Europe with you instead."

"Simple." She grins. "Don't take the SAT."

I wish. Instead, I glance between Siobhan and the quickly emptying parking lot. I parked all the way in the back. Our car is a little 2004 blue hatchback. It's not exactly a hot ride.

"I could just drive you," I say. "If your ride isn't here."

"Oh!" Siobhan glances around, like a car is suddenly going to materialize. "Well, Danny was supposed to pick me up after practice . . ."

"It's fine, then," I say. "I just don't want you to—"

"No," she says, pulling her phone out of her pocket. "Just let me—"

"Are you sure? Because—"

"It's really not a big deal—"

We pause for a second. My cheeks feel warm. Then we burst into laughter.

"Practice isn't over for at least an hour," she says, shoving her phone back into her pocket. "It would be great if you could take me home—as long as you don't mind."

I'm shaking my head too rapidly. If I were a doll, it would definitely fall off.

"No problem," I say. "Seriously. Just tell me where to go."

Where to go ends up being a cute bungalow by the water. There are two windows at the front with flower boxes underneath them. The grass is green and the sun is shining, and when the wind blows, everything smells like spring, even from inside my car. I'm almost sad to see Siobhan go.

"Thanks a ton," she says, unbuckling her seat belt. "Between my dog attacking you and this ride, I really owe you."

"You don't owe me anything," I say. "Except a trip abroad."

"Right." She nods, completely serious except for her eyes. "Of course. I'll start planning the itinerary as soon as I get inside."

"Don't forget the museums."

"I would never," she says. "How do you feel about tea?"

"Um." I blink, stumbling out of whatever we were doing back and forth. "I'm willing to try?"

She laughs, a real one, and it fills the car. Then, lightning fast, she leans over and kisses my cheek. I literally go into shock. I'm not lying. I can't move any of my body parts, even as she grabs her backpack and climbs out of the door.

"See you in history class," she says. "Maybe start saving for a down payment."

"A down payment?"

"On some hiking boots," she says, sticking out her tongue. "I've heard they can be expensive."

Then she turns and walks toward her door. I may or may not stare a little as she's walking. When she glances back, grinning at me, it feels like we're in on a secret together—like she knew I'd be watching. Or am I just imagining it? I have no clue.

I'm not even sure how I drive home after that.

* * *

My plan is to head straight to my room, call Naomi, and freak out about what just happened. But that goes out the window when I see that Mom is already home. She's on the couch, her feet up on the coffee table, taking out her French braid. I close the door quietly, but she doesn't say anything, even as I dump my backpack by my sneakers.

Something's up. Mom was supposed to be on until eight tonight. What's she doing back at three?

"H*eee*y," I say, approaching her like she's a small animal. "How was work today?"

She sits up, slowly, like she's in pain.

"Sit down, Mahalia," she says, patting the spot next to her on the couch. "I have to talk to you about something."

Oh shit. That's serious. I take a seat next to her, studying her expression. Could she be upset with me? When Mom's mad, there's yelling and folded arms and a glare that makes me hope God is real. But she's not glaring right now. She just looks . . . exhausted. I can't remember the last time she looked at me like this. Maybe when Dad didn't show up to my choir recital? But that was years ago, when I was thirteen. I haven't invited Dad to anything since then.

"What's wrong?" I say, scooting a little closer to her. "Did something bad happen?"

"Well," she says. "You know about my fibroids?"

"I do." I stare at her stomach. The idea of something being inside her, a mass of cells, sort of freaks me out. "What's going on?"

"And you remember Junior?"

I almost roll my eyes. How could I forget Mom's sentient fibroid?

"Yeah," I say. "Does your doctor have a treatment for you or something?"

"Well, yes." She won't meet my eyes. "He did an ultrasound. It's not going to get smaller on its own and it's dangerous for me."

I think back to all the times she's struggled to get comfortable on the couch or asked for ice packs and heating pads. It never freaked me out much. I just thought it was normal for someone with fibroids. Now it feels silly. I wish I could go back and pay more attention to her. Sure, Mom gets on my nerves, but I don't know what I'd do without her. I can't be without her.

My throat is dry. "Are you dying?"

"What?" She lets out a loud bark of laughter but pauses when she sees my face. I'm not laughing at all.

"Oh, baby." She grips both my hands in hers. Hers are wrinkled and coarse, probably from work, but still warm. "I'm not going anywhere until Jesus decides it's my time, and He knows how much you need me."

"Oh," I say, swallowing. "Right. That makes sense."

"I *am* going to have some pretty intense surgery," she says. "I was trying to wait as long as I could, since I didn't think I'd be able to take the time off from work, but . . . my doctor thinks I can't push it off much longer. So I'm going to have a hysterectomy and it's going to happen next Monday."

Monday. That's just a week away. After that, my mom won't have a uterus anymore.

Jesus.

On one hand, it's not like she *needs* a uterus. Mom hasn't had a kid in sixteen years. When I was little and used to ask for a sibling, she'd say I was more than enough for her, and told me to go ask my father during my visits with him. Now I have two little siblings and don't even really see them. Which is sad when you think about it.

But still. It's part of her *body.* A big part, right? I don't know how this works. Will they just yank it out of her? I shiver at the thought.

"I'm going to need your help," she continues. "It's pretty major surgery. Some people from church will be coming by, but you'll need to pull a lot of weight around here for a while. Do you understand? I'm sorry to lean on you, but I don't really have anyone else."

She shifts again, wincing, and the thought gets pushed to the back of my brain. I put a hand on her foot, rubbing.

"Don't worry about a thing, Mom," I say. "I'll take care of whatever you need."

She'll be better in time for the party. I know she'll be.

CHAPTER 12

"I'm *living.*"

"Jesus," Naomi says, shaking her head. "I don't think I've ever seen you this happy before."

I'm not the type of girl who generally gets excited about clothes, mainly because I can't afford much, so I don't even bother to look. But there's something special about being in a fancy dress shop with your best friend.

When I think of Naomi's party, I remember the dancing, the music, the food—but most of all, I remember her dress. I don't know if I have the money for something like *that*. But there's $250 free now that we aren't using a DJ, and I think I owe it to myself to try. Besides, it's nice to have something to take my mind off the bomb Mom dropped yesterday.

Naomi and I have the afternoon off, so we're at Dress Me Up, a small boutique about twenty minutes away from Naomi's house. The walls are exposed brick, the floors covered with multi-colored rugs that look like they belong in a museum—or a palace. It's designed like a showroom you'd see on *Project Runway* or something, with big gold-framed mirrors at the center of the room, surrounded by racks and racks of dresses and accessories.

It's a little bit like heaven, if I'm being truthful. I do a little magical twirl—then trip over my feet. Naomi grabs my arm to steady me.

"Let's hope no one saw that," she says under her breath, glancing toward the saleswomen standing near the entrance. They wear sleek black, from head to toe, and look like models. They probably are.

The nice thing is that there seem to be all different colors here—a group of East Asian women cooing over a dress in the corner, two Latina women gently caressing a glittering blue dress in front of the mirror, a Black woman admiring her reflection. If I knew anything about fashion, I could probably get out of taking the SAT and just work here. If only.

Naomi pulls out a cream-colored dress. It's sort of pretty, but I can't get over the embroidered flowers all over the top part. It seems like something a grandmother would wear. I shake my head.

"I need something with *flair*," I say. "Something gay."

"Well," Naomi says, frowning. "I'm not sure what a gay dress looks like . . . vulva print?"

I jab her with my elbow. To be honest, though, I'm not really sure what I mean. I want a dress that looks like something I'd wear to a Sweet Sixteen—I guess it would count as a gay dress because a gay person would be wearing it.

I pause in front of a gorgeous blue dress. The tag calls it a *ball gown silhouette*. I pull it off the rack, holding it in front of myself.

It's too long for me; more than a little bit of the skirt rests on the floor. Naomi winces.

"What?"

"It's strapless," she says. "Are you sure you want to deal with that?"

I purse my lips. I definitely have the boobs to hold it up, but there might be a little *too* much boob. Naomi probably remembers the one time I tried to wear a strapless bra and had to keep adjusting myself all day. Then I check the price tag, and my eyeballs almost fall out of my head. Four hundred and seventeen dollars for a *dress*? I put the hanger back on the rack like it burned me.

"Don't worry," Naomi says, moving on to another rack. "It's supposed to take time. Remember when we went looking for my dress?"

It's hard to forget. Naomi's mom, grandmother, and aunt all came, and we spent several hours at a dress store, watching Naomi try on different gowns and jewelry. When I told Mom afterward, she snorted a little and made a comment about it being a Sweet Sixteen, "not a damn wedding." The memory still makes me smile a little—thinking about Lady Crumbleton.

"Oh," Naomi says, pulling out another dress. "What about this one?"

Honestly, the dress is gorgeous: a pink ball gown with a thin layer of intricate embroidered baby's breath. The tag has a bunch of terms I don't get—*sweetheart neckline, A-line skirt with pleats, sweep train,* and *tulle overlay*—but they make it seem even more like a princess dress. It's love at first sight.

I hold it over my body, but before I see Naomi's face, I can already tell there's a problem. She starts rapidly pushing hangers to the side.

"Hold on," she says. "There might be another size."

But there isn't. We search the entire rack, then ask one of the women at the front, but there isn't a dress big enough for me. The sleek, slim woman looks me up and down.

"Maybe," she says, "you can try Lane Bryant."

"That's actually not really helpful." Naomi narrows her eyes. "Is your manager here?"

Normally, I'd laugh at her for doing this—Naomi and her mother are very good at playing the part of Karen. But right now I just want to leave the store. If there's a perfect dress for me, it definitely isn't here.

* * *

Naomi guesses that a trip to Target will make me feel better. She is correct. I mope on the car ride over, but as soon as we step foot inside, I'm revived by the spirit of consumerism and practically run toward the party section.

"These?" I pick up a pack of pink party invitations. "What do you think?"

Naomi wrinkles her nose. I nod, tossing them back. The aisles are stuffed with confetti and streamers and balloons, but I'm not necessarily thinking about decorations.

"Oh," I say, reaching for a different pack. "What about these?"

It's a pastel background with pink, purple, blue, and yellow blending together. *You're invited* is written in gold cursive, stars dotted around the words.

"Definitely better," Naomi says. "I'd get a few extra, just in case."

"Cool." I grab at least five packs. "Do you know when I'm supposed to send them out?"

"Well." Naomi rubs the back of her neck. "My mom says you're supposed to hand-deliver the invitations for a Sweet Sixteen. But I don't know if this really counts?"

Now that she mentions it, I do remember Naomi walking around in the cafeteria during lunch and in classrooms before the bell rang, discreetly slipping envelopes to guests. People whispered about it the entire day. But my party won't have the same impact—it'll mostly be Naomi, her family, and a few other classmates I sometimes talk to.

"Do you remember when I was nervous to give Cody his invitation?" Naomi laughs awkwardly. "It sounds kind of corny, but I thought about doing something like that again. Like writing a note about my feelings and giving it to him."

A note? What century is this?

"I don't know." I shrug, still holding the packs to my chest. "Sounds like a lot of work."

"Yeah," Naomi says, nodding a little too hard. "You're right."

We step through the aisle, looking at mini containers of bubbles, suction-cup balls, toy mustaches. None of them seem like a good fit for my party. I'm not sure what I'm looking for, exactly, but I know this isn't it. When I asked Naomi to come shopping with me, I figured she'd be full of advice, pointing out which supplies I'd need and which to ditch. But she's quieter than I expected her to be. I pause in front of a bunch of colorful sashes meant for birthdays and bachelorette parties. I turn to Naomi.

"Do you think I should try to get those candles like you did?"

Everyone who went to Naomi's party left with a little pink candle emblazoned with a crown and *Naomi's Sweet Sixteen* on the front. When I lit it at home, it smelled like strawberries.

"I don't know," Naomi says, glancing at a pack of string lights. "My mom actually came up with that. I can ask her where she got them done, though."

Something is definitely off with her. I'm about to say something when I spot them—packs of mini spiral notebooks with a serene-looking unicorn and *Sparkle Wherever You Go* in rainbow capital letters on the front. It's one of the gayest things I've ever seen.

"Fuck, Naomi," I say, holding up a pack. "Aren't these perfect?"

Her face splits into a grin. She grabs the pack from my hand.

"Yeah," she says, nodding. "These are pretty amazing."

I start grabbing as many packs as I can hold in my arms. Naomi looks up, eyebrows furrowing.

"Wait," she says. "How many are you gonna need?"

She has a point. I start to put some of the packs back.

"I don't know," I say. "I budgeted for twenty, but maybe . . ."

I trail off as Naomi starts grabbing my packs and tossing them back on the shelf.

"Well, how much did the venue charge you for the deposit?"

Since the venue visit with Mom didn't work out, I ended up finding a place on an app that rents out different types of space for meetings and parties and stuff. It's only $525 for three hours in a gigantic, warehouse-like space that I'm sure I can fix up with the right decorations. The only annoying part is that the payment is due super early—at the end of May, even though I picked a July date for the party.

"It's not really a deposit. I have to pay the whole bill," I say. "Here, take these."

She obediently opens out her arms, but she's still frowning, even when I pick out a pink tiara and balance it on top of her head. This isn't working for me. She's supposed to be having fun.

"What?" I finally say. "Do you think the tiara is too much?"

"I mean," she says. "How long is it gonna take you to save?"

I bristle a little bit.

"I literally can pay it as soon as I get my next paycheck."

"But what about your other expenses?" She tilts her head to the side. "Like gas and food and stuff? Your phone?"

"It's going to be fine," I say, wandering to the next aisle. "I don't have to pay the bill until the end of May. That's literally a whole month."

This aisle has tableware and piñatas and candles. There are big colored numbers and birthday candles, but there are also different letters and shapes, like a unicorn cake topper and a pack of glittering pink hearts.

"Do you see any rainbows?" I ask. "Or anything else gay?"

"Uhhh . . ." Naomi scans the aisle. "Magical Princess Toppers?"

"That sounds like a gigantic innuendo."

I step toward them, but they're pretty basic: pale colors, blank little doll faces. Not enough flair.

"How about the flamingo?" I ask, pulling it off the hook. "Wrong vibe?"

"I think it's fine," Naomi says, picking up another container. "And then just get some letter candles."

With our hands stuffed, walking to the register is a literal balancing act. I keep making funny faces at Naomi over the pile of supplies reaching up to my chin. She doesn't laugh, but she does roll her eyes and shake her head.

"Maybe," Naomi says, "a cart would've been a good idea."

"Maybe," I say. "But where's the fun in that?"

-$40 for gas
-$20 for pizza
GOAL: $704

CHAPTER 13

After her surgery, Mom has to stay in the hospital for two days.

Greta gives me the days off when I tell her about my situation—and also gives me some healing crystals to give to Mom. The first day, I'm not at school, I'm at the hospital, talking to her about nothing or watching soap operas on the TV she shares with another patient. Most of the drugs make her fall asleep. It's pretty boring.

"You should let me come visit," Naomi says when I tell her about it at lunch on Tuesday.

I don't know if it's a bad idea or not. Mom is pretty out of it. I know the nurses are giving her medication, but I don't know what type. She won't be able to drive until she's not taking them anymore and the doctor said that could take two weeks. Someone from church is supposed to take her home tomorrow. She might not want Naomi to see her dozing off every few minutes.

Then again, Naomi's basically family, and it'll be nice not to feel so alone. For a little bit after our Target run last week, things felt weird. But if Naomi still feels the weirdness, I can't see it in her expression.

"Okay," I say, stealing some of her sandwich. "Let's do it."

Since Naomi still has to head to work, I drive to the hospital and she follows behind me in her own car. I sort of wish I hadn't driven to school today so we could ride together. It seems like I'm alone everywhere: at home, at the hospital, in my bed at night when it's time to go to sleep. I haven't even been thinking about Siobhan as much as usual. Our research for the group project in history ended, so I mostly glance at her while she giggles with Danny, then hate myself at the end of the period.

The recovery floor has a nurses' station out front, where we have to stop to get Naomi's visitor's pass. I wish my mom worked in a hospital like this. Everything is bright and sunny. Behind the desk, there are pictures of the different nurses dressed up in costumes, maybe from a party.

"Well, you're all set, ladies," the nurse at the desk says, handing Naomi a pass. "Have a nice day."

"You too," Naomi says, with her pretty voice and bright grin.

Mom's room is in the middle of the hall. I hear a voice drifting out into the hallway as I approach. At first, I'm sure it's the other patient who shares the room, but the other bed is empty. When I turn my head to the side, I see my father sitting in the chair next to her.

"Well, well, well," he says, turning toward us. "If it isn't the Queen!"

I freeze.

I haven't seen my dad since my birthday back in February. Mom and I have a tradition of going out to eat at Winnie's, the best soul food place ever, and we shared an entire cake afterward. Dad was waiting outside our apartment when we got home. He gave me a card and a kiss and tried to stick around, but it was too awkward. It always is.

The worst part is that I look just like him. I know it because everyone says it, but it's a little creepy to see yourself reflected in someone you don't feel close to. We have the same narrow eyes, big lips, and button nose. Dad just smiles better than me. His smile is what made Mom—and I guess Jada, his girlfriend—go weak in the knees.

I should practice in the mirror to see if I can use the family smile to win over Siobhan.

He rests his hands on his knees, leaning forward with that signature smile, like he's waiting for me to run over and give him a kiss on the cheek or something. But I just stand in the doorway and blink at him.

"Naomi," Mom says, cutting through the silence. "It's so nice to see you, honey! But don't you have work today?"

I glance at my mother. She's sitting up in bed, more lucid than I've seen her since the operation. Her hands are folded over her stomach despite the tubes attached to her arms. She almost looks like she's holding court or something. I wonder what she and my father could've been talking about.

"Oh yeah," Naomi says. "I just wanted to check and make sure that you're okay. My parents said they're around to help with whatever you need."

It's true. Once they found out about the surgery, they even offered to let me stay over while Mom was in the hospital. I surprised myself by saying no. A strange part of me figured that if Mom hadn't asked them to keep me, she didn't want me at their house. And another, more protective part wanted to be at the hospital as much as I could. I'm sure Mr. and Mrs. Sanders wouldn't have given me a hard time about visiting, but I would've felt out of place watching them all eat dinner together, joke together, just *be* together. It's lonely by myself, but at least I'm not constantly reminded of what I don't have.

"That's so kind of you," Mom says, smiling. "Please send them my thanks. And come on in, girls. I don't want you standing by the door like strangers."

Naomi starts to walk forward, and I take a few steps behind her. I'm not really sure where we're supposed to go. Dad already took my seat.

"Damn, Naomi," he says. "You're so big! The last time I saw you, you must've been up to here."

He holds his hand against his waist. Naomi laughs, but I'm probably the only one who can tell it's forced. I can't stop staring at him.

"What are you doing here?" I blurt out.

"Mahalia," Mom says, although she doesn't *sound* that upset.

"No, it's all right," Dad says, waving a hand. "Your mother told me she was gonna be having some surgery. I know you already stayed at home alone yesterday, but I want to be around to help out more, and we were talking about some ways I could do that."

"Oh."

I look between the two of them. Mom's face doesn't tell me anything, so I'm not sure what *help out more* means. He already pays child support. It's not a lot, according to Mom, but it's what the judge ordered. She puts it toward rent every month. Is that what he's talking about? Giving us more money?

"And look," Dad says, leaning forward again. "I was thinking you could stay with me and Jada and the kids. So you're not alone."

"I was already alone," I say. "Last night."

His smile drops a bit.

"Well, I got the dates mixed up a little," he says, rubbing the back of his head. "But you could always stay tonight. I know you haven't been around the house much, but—"

"I think it's okay," I say, folding my arms. "Mom comes home tomorrow and I've stayed home alone when she's had overnight shifts. I'm fine."

Dad glances at Mom. She lifts her shoulders in a small shrug.

"Um," Naomi says, clearing her throat. "I'm sorry to interrupt, but I have to head to work pretty soon."

"Oh yeah," I say. "I should come with you."

"Are you sure?" Dad says. "I could drop you off—"

"Thanks, Mr. Hynes," Naomi says, pulling at her backpack strap. "But I've got a car."

I pull her into a sideways hug. I love her.

"Well," Dad says, glancing between the two of us. "Come back after you've said goodbye, Hallie. I want to talk about how I can help out while your mother is recovering."

I nod as we back out of the room, not bothering to tell him that he's the only one who still calls me by my old nickname. Naomi waits until we're down in the lobby before she says anything.

"That was awkward, huh?"

"God, extremely," I say, shaking my head. "And I'm gonna have to go back for more."

"Oof." Naomi places a hand on my shoulder. "Godspeed."

It's stupid, but after she's gone I sit in my car for like fifteen minutes, just to get out of that room. It's weird enough to see my parents together, but with Mom in the hospital, it's even weirder. Like an alternate universe where they never broke up. What would life be like then? I don't even know how to imagine that.

I start playing Bowie to psych myself up, but it's not working the way it usually does. It's stupid to avoid my dad like this. Mom was asleep most of yesterday, and today is my first real day with her, so at the very least I shouldn't waste it. With a sigh, I force myself to go back into the hospital.

But when I get back to Mom's room, he's nowhere to be found.

"Um," I say, glaring down at his seat. The one he stole from me. "Where did Dad go?"

Mom bites her lip so quickly I'm not sure I've actually seen it.

"An emergency," she says. "Reign got sick at school."

Reign, my half sister, is only five. She's little. I shouldn't be mad at a five-year-old. I'm *not* mad at a five-year-old. But I'm slightly pissed at my dad, even though I was the one avoiding him. Wasn't he just talking about wanting to help? Then he left before I even got back.

"Don't be upset," Mom says. "You know he has responsibilities . . ."

I want to snap at her then. If he has a responsibility to his younger kids, he has a responsibility to me, too. Especially now that Mom is in the hospital. But this isn't the first time something like this has happened. It probably won't be the last, either. I force myself to take a deep breath.

"I know," I say through clenched teeth.

Mom pats the spot next to her. I glance at the door, but there's no sign of a nurse or doctor, so I snuggle myself on the hospital bed next to her. She rests a hand on my head.

"I'm sorry, baby," she whispers.

I turn my head into the crook of her neck and breathe deep. Mom's always been here and she always will be. That's one thing I don't have to worry about.

CHAPTER 14

"I'm sorry, sir," I say, even though I'm not really sorry at all. "But I've tried five times. I don't think the card is working."

"Try it again," the man says, running a hand through his hair. "It has to work. I was just talking to the bank this morning."

I hold back my sigh. It's Thursday and I'm back at work. I need the hours to save for my party, since my savings have been dwindling, but I definitely wish I were still at home. I swipe the card again and the screen tells me it's declined. I hand the card back to the man, trying not to glance at the fifty dollars' worth of groceries I've already bagged up.

"I'm sorry," I say again. "Do you have another card?"

"Goddammit," he snaps, loud enough for me to jump. "No, I do *not* have another card. This one has to work."

I'm quitting this job the moment the party is over.

"Is everything okay here?" Bill says, walking over. Thank God.

"Actually, this man's card isn't working," I say, handing the card to Bill. "I've tried six times."

"Oh no," Bill says, frowning down at it. He looks back up at the man with a smile. "Let's see if I can help you out."

I slink away before he can ask me to do anything else.

Naomi and another employee are at the other cash registers. Someone else is already tending the organic fruits. This leaves nothing but my favorite job: standing around and pretending like I'm doing something important. In other words, randomly arranging produce in a part of the store where there's the least amount of people, next to a Wet Floor sign.

"Eek!"

One minute this woman is walking while staring down at her phone and the next she's slipped in the puddle, falling flat on her ass, knocking over a stream of apples, pears, and oranges in the process. A bark of laughter escapes my lips before I can slap my hand over my mouth. It's too late. She glares at me, face red, eyes wide. I can't tell if she's about to scream at me or not.

"Mahalia."

Shit. I turn to see Greta shaking her head at me. She walks over to the customer and presses a hand against her shoulder, helping her stand up.

"I'm so sorry," she says in a low murmur, like she's trying to soothe a scared animal. "Come on, let me help you."

The two of them stand. Greta throws a severe look my way.

"Sorry," I say. The edges of my mouth are twitching. God, I'm horrible. "I'm really sorry you fell. And for laughing."

The woman doesn't look amused.

"Mahalia," Greta says. "I'd like to see you in my office."

Shit.

The last time I was called to Greta's office was when I used my phone on the job, way back when I first got hired. After a lecture that seemed to last forever about the dangers of 5G waves, I never made that mistake again.

The office is at the back of the store and smells like patchouli oil and chia seeds. Greta has dream catchers hanging in here for some reason and paintings of landscapes on the walls. There's so much incense burning, I'm pretty sure it's a fire hazard.

After a minute or two of waiting, Greta appears. I swallow.

"Mahalia," she says. "I think you know why you're here."

I squirm uncomfortably in my seat.

"Instead of laughing at a customer, maybe you could've alerted her to the Wet Floor sign before something unfortunate happened. Isn't that what you would've wanted someone to do if you'd been in Stacy's position?"

Stacy? Somehow they became best friends within the last five minutes. It's like Greta has this weird power over people. White people, anyway.

"I understand," I say, trying to sound as serious as possible. "I'm sorry. I reacted without thinking. I didn't mean to be rude to a customer."

Greta stares at me for a long time. I get uncomfortable staring into her green eyes—they remind me of weed, for some reason, like she's been smoking a lot of it.

"I know you must be going through a rough time," she finally says. "With your mother's surgery and all. But I've noticed a decline in your work performance these last few weeks, and I have to tell you that I'm not very thrilled."

Fuck. I scan my memories, trying to remember the last time I acted out when Greta was around, but I can't think of any.

Maybe she's noticed how much time I spend at Naomi's register, talking about girls instead of working. Maybe she's noticed how much help I need from Bill. Or maybe she was watching me stand around and do nothing before that woman—*Stacy*—fell.

Whatever it was, I guess it doesn't really matter now. My throat feels dry.

"Greta," I say. "I'm so sorry. It's been a rough time, you know? But I'll do better."

"I know you will," she says. "Because I'm putting you on probation."

My heart drops into the pit of my stomach. Shit.

"I'm cutting your shifts down for the next few weeks," she continues, shuffling papers on her desk. "You can shadow Bill."

"You can't do that," I blurt out. "I need the shifts."

Greta glances up, raising a brow. For the first time in a while, she doesn't look like a silly hippie, someone I spend most of my shifts laughing at. She's my boss—my boss who will fire me if I don't get my shit together.

"I think this will be good for you, Mahalia," she says, placing a hand on my shoulder. "And in the meantime, I would encourage you to do some soul-searching. It's troublesome that your first instinct was to laugh at someone when they were at their lowest point."

Part of me wants to yell at her. Isn't she doing the same thing to me?

"Sure. I'll definitely do some reflecting," I say. "But are you sure there isn't any way—"

"You'll start shadowing Bill tomorrow," she says, turning

back to her desk. "I'm going to have to dock your pay. But you can finish the rest of your shift today."

With a sigh, I leave the office, pausing outside. My eyes burn with unshed tears. God. Why is everything so fucking hard? I force myself back to my register. There aren't even any customers in line. Figures.

"Hey," Naomi says. "What's wrong with you?"

"I'm on probation."

"Seriously?" She blinks, eyes widening. "*Greta* put you on *probation*?"

I run through the story for her, even though thinking about it just makes me want to cry again. Which is stupid. This job isn't worth crying about. Greta being unimpressed with my work ethic isn't anything to cry about. But losing my extra shifts is.

"Fuck, Mahalia," Naomi says, shaking her head. "I'm sorry."

"It's whatever," I say, even though I know I'm pouting.

Naomi's eyes dart back and forth like someone's spying on us before she pulls out her phone and glances at herself in the camera. I glare down at the conveyor belt in front of me. I kind of want to text Mom about this, but I don't want to disappoint her, and frankly I don't need the lecture. I can picture her watching Tyler Perry movies on the couch, half asleep, then furiously typing a response to me when she hears about what a bad worker I am.

I sigh again. Loudly. Naomi kisses her teeth.

"Can you tell me if my eyebrows look good?"

"What?"

"My eyebrows," she repeats. "Do they need to be done?"

"Um," I say. "They look like eyebrows. How is this making me feel better?"

Naomi stares at me like I just said I didn't know who the president was.

"What?"

"I have a Key Club thing tomorrow," she says slowly.

"Okay?"

"Cody's in Key Club," Naomi says. "I just want to look nice."

Oh.

If I were closer, I'd playfully shove her shoulder or something, but I'm honestly afraid to leave my station. Instead, I shake my head at her.

"Naomi," I say. "You look fine."

"Fine?" She laughs a little. "Just fine?"

I'm about to say something else when someone walks over and Naomi pastes on her customer service smile. I blink.

It can't be—Siobhan?

It feels like I haven't seen her in months, even though we're in class every day. The last time we hung out, just the two of us, was two weeks ago at the dog park. It feels like it's been so much longer.

Mom's friends from church helped get her settled at home and left us tons of food, but that still leaves me to take care of her—adjusting her pillows, giving her medication, reheating her food. Without my free period and lunch, I have no idea how I'd get any homework done.

I'm almost expecting Siobhan to be pissed that I ditched her, but she's smiling at me like she's shy.

"Hey," I say. My voice cracks. "How are you?"

"Great," she says. She's wearing overalls and it's pretty cute. "I'm sorry, but I don't actually have anything I need to buy."

"It's not a problem," Naomi says, glancing back. Bill and Greta are nowhere to be found. "As long as you don't linger, I think we'll be fine. What's up? How have you been adjusting?"

"It's definitely a lot warmer here," she says, glancing between the two of us. Her gaze lingers a little bit on me. "And the accents are different, of course."

She's different than before. More guarded. Maybe because Naomi is here?

"Of course," I say, laughing awkwardly. "Your accent is so cool. It's like—actually, wait, no."

"Like what?" Siobhan cocks her head to the side. "Now I have to know."

Even Naomi looks at me with a question in her expression.

"I was going to say like Shrek," I say. "But I know—"

Siobhan breaks into shrieking laughter. Naomi is giggling, too, but she's definitely not as loud. A few customers actually turn to look.

"It was just a random thought!" I say, but my face is warm in a good way. "I shouldn't have said it."

"That's so kind of you," Siobhan says, holding her stomach. "To compare my lovely accent to the dulcet, calming tones of *Shrek*."

"Listen." I hold my hands up. "I happen to be a big fan of Shrek, so think of it as a compliment."

"I'll have you know," Siobhan says, her face red from laughter, "Shrek actually has a *Scottish* accent. I'm Irish. Have you forgotten already?"

"Is there a difference?"

"Mahalia." Siobhan's voice goes deathly quiet. "I'm now required, by law, to challenge you to a duel."

"Yikes," I say. "Do you think you can duel in Birkenstocks or should we find you some sneakers?"

Siobhan grins. I think she's about to say something else when Naomi coughs. My cheeks burn. I wish I could dig my elbow into her side or at least stomp on her foot.

"Anyway," Siobhan says, shifting awkwardly. "I was just in the neighborhood and I thought I'd pop by and see if you guys wanted to come over and maybe study sometime, maybe one day after work? The SAT is next week and I was thinking I could use the practice. I know it's—"

"Yes," I say. "We'd totally like to come."

Naomi turns to stare at me, but I'm not looking at her. I'm looking at Siobhan, who smiles back like it's the best thing she's heard all day. That's all I need.

CHAPTER 15

It's Friday and we're outside Siobhan's house for what's supposed to be a study date. I don't know why I'm so freaked out. After all, I've been here before. I've just never actually been *inside*. And I haven't hung out with Siobhan in a bit. What if I forget how to talk?

Before I can say anything, Naomi rings the bell. There goes my chance to run.

"Naomi—" I start.

A loud bark interrupts me. The door swings open and Naomi is practically tackled by Doodle. Her tongue lolls out and leaves a trail of slobber behind on Naomi's cheek. Ew. Naomi doesn't even seem to mind. She tries to grab the dog's paws with one hand while rubbing her head with the other.

"Oh, hi," she coos, rubbing Doodle's head. "How are you?"

"Jeez, Doodle," I say. "I thought we had something."

Siobhan appears in the door, cheeks flushed, grinning.

"Hey!" she says. "Sorry about that. Doodle can get, well, pretty excited."

That's an understatement.

Doodle follows me into the living room, where the three of us sit on the couch. Doodle doesn't seem to realize she's too big to sit in my lap, because she tries anyway, leaving me without any room to take out the SAT workbook I got from the discount section of Target. Oh well.

"Where are your parents?" I ask, trying to situate Doodle. "Are they spying on us from afar?"

"No spying, sadly," Siobhan says, smirking. "They don't get home until a little later."

I'm so used to Naomi's parents being around all the time that it didn't occur to me Siobhan's parents might work a ton, like my mom. At least this is a nice place to be alone. The couch is soft and comfortable. The TV is hidden in a wooden cupboard. A multicolored rug covers the floor. The room smells like vanilla candles. The whole thing is so cozy.

"Okay," Naomi says. "I figured we could start with the reading portion. Mahalia is good at that and I'm totally not."

"Oh yeah," Siobhan says. "I'm not the best at grammar, either."

"It's just easy to me." I shrug a little. "I don't really think about it. I just figure out what sounds right and what doesn't."

"No studying any rules?" Siobhan asks, raising her brows. "I drive myself crazy trying to keep everything straight."

"It's just like you're proofreading something," I say. "Have you ever had to trade essays with someone in class? Like that."

"Listen to her." Naomi rolls her eyes. "She makes it sound so easy."

"Maybe we can start with the math?" I say, flipping to the back of my workbook. "That's where I'm completely fucking lost."

"I'm afraid I'm not the best at that, either," Siobhan says.

She has printed-out sheets of a practice test on her lap and holds them up for us to see. They're covered in crossed-out answers and scribbled-out notes.

"Finally, someone who understands me," I say, bumping shoulders with Naomi. "She thinks all this stuff is easy. Doesn't even use a calculator."

"The hard part is just remembering all the formulas," Naomi says, shaking her head. "Come on. I'll show both of you guys."

She bends down to dig through her backpack, probably checking for texts. I turn to kiss the top of Doodle's head. What can I say? She's grown on me.

"Way to make me feel jealous," Siobhan mumbles.

My head snaps up. When I meet her eyes, she quickly looks away, a shy smile on her face.

Is this how flirting works? I'm pretty sure it is. But she shouldn't be flirting with me if she has a *boyfriend*. God. Bible Camp Isabel was a hundred times less complicated than this.

I've always felt like boys were being dramatic when they talked about how confusing girls can be. Girls, in general, aren't confusing. You just talk to them and you can figure them out pretty quickly, just like you would with any person. But Siobhan is the most confusing person I've ever met.

"Okay," Naomi says. "So, linear inequalities?"

Naomi goes over different algebra problems with us. I'm not *bad* at math, exactly. I just can't do it as fast as Naomi. When she starts timing us on the practice questions, it takes me forever to get through even one, and I don't have time for the rest. But then, on my second try, I start skipping through problems and just circling random answers because I'm so freaked out about the time.

"This is *impossible*," I groan, dramatically sinking myself back against the couch. "I'm going to fail."

"I don't think you *can* fail," Siobhan says. "That's positive, right?"

I bite my lip, trying to hide my smile.

"Let me rephrase, then," I say. "I doubt I'll get a high enough score to get scholarships."

"I told you to practice the math questions earlier," Naomi says, flipping through my practice questions, fixing them with a red pen like a teacher. "Studying the week before isn't exactly going to help."

My skin goes hot.

"I *have* been working on it," I say. "It just doesn't come natural to me."

"I don't think a timed test comes natural to anyone," Naomi says. Then she glances up and seems to realize what she said. "Don't worry. I'm probably going to mostly guess on the reading portion."

I know she's just trying to make me feel better. Naomi's parents put her in SAT Prep class—and it's only her first try.

"You could always take it again," Siobhan offers. "If I go the college route, I might take it five times, or until they stop letting me sign up."

"Yeah, well, I don't know how many times I can pay fifty-five bucks for a test."

"Oh, that's true." Siobhan's eyebrows knit together. "But they have the waivers—"

I shake my head. I don't want to get into this with her—how they only give you a waiver if you get free lunch, and I don't qualify because my mom makes like five hundred dollars more than the cutoff. I honestly regret bringing up money in the first place. Siobhan doesn't need to know this stuff. It's just embarrassing.

Doodle comes running back over, nudging my hand. I rest it on her head.

"Maybe," Naomi adds after a moment, "you can use some of your party money to sign up for an SAT class next time."

"Party money?" Siobhan glances over at me. "A party for what?"

I kind of want to strangle Naomi. Why would she bring that up right now, in front of Siobhan? I don't know why I'm so self-conscious. Maybe it's because I don't know whether or not Siobhan is queer. If she isn't, will she think I'm weird for trying to do this? I don't want to risk it. I want to keep that fuzzy feeling in my chest that appears whenever I spend time with her.

"It's just, you know, like a belated Sweet Sixteen," I say. "And yeah, maybe I'll use what's left over to sign up for a class or something."

"*Or . . .*"—Naomi rubs the back of her head—"you could postpone the party."

I blink at her. The party was practically *her* idea. Why is she changing her mind all of a sudden?

"Why?" I cock my head to the side. "I have time. The party will be in July and I can take the SAT in the fall. I don't need to give up the party for that."

"Well, I know," Naomi says. "But with your mom and everything . . ."

"Naomi." I close my SAT workbook. "I really don't want to talk about this."

"Uh," Siobhan says, "maybe it's time for a break."

I keep staring at Naomi, who suddenly won't meet my eye. I want to ask what her problem is. She sure seems to have a lot of *suggestions* about how I should spend my money when she doesn't have to worry about any of the same things that I do. And I'd say all of that—if we weren't at Siobhan's house. It's almost like she brought it up in front of Siobhan so that I couldn't argue back.

What a shitty thing to do.

"Actually," Naomi says, glancing down at her phone, "I think I should get going. I can't be late to dinner."

"Oh," I say. Her family has dinner at six every night. It's a *thing*. "I forgot about that."

"Are you coming?"

I hesitate. Part of me wants to chew her out in the car ride there, but I don't want to sit at the table and pretend like everything is fine afterward. I don't want to be reminded of everything she has. And I don't want to feel like a jealous asshole, even though I know that's what I am.

Then there's the fact that I'm at *Siobhan's*. How many times will I get to do this—be alone with her, at her actual house?

"Uh," I say. "I can probably find my own way home."

"Are you sure?" Naomi's eyebrows shoot up. "Where are you gonna eat?"

"We have food here, you know," Siobhan says, a laugh in her voice. "My parents probably won't come home until around 7:30. It's a late day for both of them. But if you can wait until then, you can eat with us, and maybe one of them can drive you home."

If I stay here, I'm gonna have to talk to her parents. Parents are scary. Sure, Naomi's parents like me, but I've known them forever. I'm not sure how to charm new parents at all.

I clear my throat. "You can't drive?"

"No," Siobhan says. "I wasn't old enough in Dublin. But my parents can."

"I mean," Naomi says, packing up her bag. "I guess I'll just go home. Alone. All by myself."

I almost want to apologize and go with her. Almost. But she never should have brought up my money problems in front of Siobhan.

"You have four other people living in that house," I say, nudging her. "Siobhan will make sure I get home safe."

Naomi stares hard at her backpack.

"Don't worry," Siobhan says, tossing an arm around my shoulders. My skin tingles at the contact. "I'll take good care of Mahalia."

Jesus. I might just die. I have to learn how to stop freaking out every time she does something normal like saying my name, but it could quite possibly take forever.

"Fine," Naomi says, swinging her backpack on. "I'll see you later."

"I'll walk you out," Siobhan says, getting up.

I should probably get up and walk my best friend to the door, but I'm too busy freaking out about the fact that I'm alone with Siobhan. Doodle perks up and heads toward the door and gives Naomi a goodbye kiss.

"Traitor," I mutter.

"Okay," Siobhan says, whirling back into the room and plopping on the couch. "I'm sorry to see her go, but I'm actually really glad for the break. There's only so much I can listen to about the SAT."

"But our *future*," I say. "*College.* All of that incredibly important . . . can you tell that thinking about this makes me want to throw up?"

She snorts a little.

"I feel the exact same. My head hurts. Let's talk about something else. Anything else."

Doodle jumps up on the couch between the two of us. Siobhan rubs her head. This feels so normal, it makes my heart ache in this weird way it never has before.

"How are things with Danny?"

If I sound petty, Siobhan can't tell. She scrunches her face as she thinks, freckles disappearing into the little crinkles around her eyes.

"Good," she says, tossing her head to the side. Some of her hair spills out against the couch. "I'm actually really glad I have him, you know? He knows a lot of people and he's helped to introduce me to the community. I don't feel like such a sore thumb."

"Yeah," I say. "That sounds really good."

Actually, it sounds more like a business transaction to me, but I'm not going to say that. Maybe that's why we don't actually feel like *friends*. If this were Naomi sitting in front of me, I'd tell her to dump him because Danny is annoying as hell, but I'd also tell her she doesn't really sound that into him. I definitely know what crushes are like. I'm suffering through one right now.

"And I think our project is going to go really well," Siobhan says. "I've looked at the Google Slides you already started to put together and they're amazing."

I doubt that—I've just taken the work we've done separately and added images.

"It's probably what everyone else will be doing," I say, rubbing the back of my neck. "Not a big deal or anything."

"Well, count *me* as impressed." She nudges my foot. "Do you want to look for something to watch on YouTube?"

I follow her down a hallway, trying to shove my feelings into my gut so I don't accidentally barf them all over her.

CHAPTER 16

"Oh *man*."

I'm twirling around Siobhan's living room. "Dreams" by Fleetwood Mac is blasting on her laptop. It feels like I'm one with the universe. Greta would be proud.

"Wow," Siobhan says. "Do you like this old stuff? This is what my mum listens to."

"It's classic," I say, waving my arms like I'm a squid. "This really takes me back."

"Back *when*?"

"Back to a better time." I can't stop the twitch of a smile on my lips. "A time before I can remember."

Siobhan throws her head back and laughs. It's not soft and sunny like the rest of her. It's a cackle—sort of how you'd think a witch from Ireland would sound. Not that I'm calling her a witch from Ireland. It almost catches me off guard, but then I'm laughing with her.

"Come on," I say, pulling her off the couch. "Get into it. Twirl into the Earth."

"Mahalia, *what* are you going on about?"

I twirl her around and she laughs and laughs and laughs. I'm dizzy.

Doodle interrupts the moment by barking. She comes out of nowhere, running over to the door. The sound of a key turning is almost as loud as the song. After a second, two people shuffle inside. I stop spinning Siobhan.

The man has long dreads twisted up into a bun on top of his head. He looks younger than Naomi's dad but older than my mother. It's always hard to tell how old Black people are. He greets me with a grin.

"Well, well, well," he says in a warm voice, turning to the woman next to him. "Katie, it looks like we missed a pretty groovy dance party."

"*Groovy?*" Siobhan repeats. "Dad, please stop revealing your age."

She sways a bit on her feet, leaning into me. I try to hide my intense glee.

"Ah," the woman says. "You must be Mahalia."

There's the accent. It makes her sound younger than she looks. Her hair is short like a pixie cut. She has freckles like Siobhan's.

"Yeah," I say, clearing my throat. "That's me."

Her dad steps toward me, holding out a hand.

"Mahalia," he repeats, trying the name out. "Just like the Queen."

"Yeah," I say, shaking his hand. "Not many people get that."

Most often it's Black people who recognize that I'm named after a gospel singer (*the* gospel singer, seriously, the best one of all time), especially *older* Black people. Siobhan smiles next to me.

"It's nice to meet you, Mahalia," her mom says, sweeping me into a hug. She smells like cut grass. "You can call me Katie. And that knucklehead over there is my husband, Terrence."

She pulls back, taking a look at me. There's a grin on her face.

"I've heard so much about you," she says, squeezing my shoulders. "I haven't heard Siobhan talk about anyone like this since Erin."

"*Mum,*" Siobhan snaps. "Seriously?"

My gay senses start tingling.

"Erin?" I repeat. "Who is that?"

"No one," Siobhan says.

"Our neighbor back in Dublin," Katie says at the same time. "Siobhan had a wee crush."

Oh. My. God. She had a crush on a girl?

"*Mum,*" Siobhan hisses. Her face is all red.

"Honestly," Katie says. "What's the problem?"

Terrence claps his hands together.

"What do you ladies say about grilling something for dinner?" he asks, gesturing outside. "Kabobs?"

Siobhan is too busy glaring at her mother to answer. I feel like jumping up and down. Sure, there's the chance her mother is kidding, or somehow making fun of her. But it doesn't seem like she is. It sounds like Siobhan is actually queer.

"Yeah!" I say, way too loud. "I love kabobs."

"They'll be meat-free," Siobhan says. "We're a vegetarian household."

I glance over at her, but she won't meet my eyes. Maybe she's embarrassed. I want to squeeze her hand and tell her she shouldn't be. "Anything in kabob form is fine with me," I tell her.

Terrence flashes me a smile. "Care to join us outside, girls?"

Siobhan doesn't look at me as we're walking outside. Sometimes I catch her glancing at me over dinner, but she quickly looks away. The food is great, but my stomach still twists, nervous about what this means for the future of our friendship.

She *talks* about me. She had a crush on a girl named Erin. That has to mean something. The question is whether it's something good or something bad.

* * *

I'm sitting in the backseat of this small, clean car with Siobhan, who looks like she's trying not to make eye contact. Her mom won't stop asking questions from the driver's seat. The only thing that could make this worse would be if I were sitting in the front seat.

"So, Mahalia," Siobhan's mom says, turning down another street. Thank God we're close to my apartment building. I've never wanted to get out of a car faster. "What do you think you want to be when you grow up?"

"Uh," I say. "I don't really know."

I hate when adults ask this. They want us to be children and adults at the same time. They want us to be good at school and do a shit ton of stuff outside of it just so we can go to college—even if we don't want to—and join the world of the rest of them, who only complain about their jobs and debt and taxes all day.

"Oh, I'm sure that's not true," Siobhan's mom says, waving

her hand. "You're a junior, aren't you? You have to have some sort of idea. Where are you going to apply to college in the fall?"

I cough a little too loudly.

"Uh," I say. "Well. Um. College. How about that?"

"Mum," Siobhan cuts in. "It's not a job interview."

"I'm just trying to make conversation!"

"No, it's totally fine," I say. "I mean, the *hope* is to study communication at UC San Diego. I really want to work in radio, and it's close to home, so . . ."

It's not the first time I've told someone this, but it always feels like a big deal whenever I do. Like saying it out loud makes it even more real—like something I can really fuck up. UC San Diego isn't as competitive as some of the other UCs, but it's still a big deal. My grades are good. I have a job, showing how responsible I can be, or whatever. But I'm not the type of applicant with a million clubs on my resume. And if I don't figure out a way to get a good score on the SAT . . .

"How exciting is that!" Katie says. "It's so amazing to see a young person already know what they want. It takes the rest of us a bit longer, doesn't it, Siobhan?"

I try to make out Siobhan's expression in the dark, but I can barely see it. Then she looks up and meets my eyes in the mirror. With her gaze pinned on me, I can't look away. What does it mean? It feels intimate, even though we aren't speaking.

"It was lovely having you for dinner, Mahalia," Katie says, stopping the car. "I hope we see you over again soon."

Siobhan looks away and I immediately feel the absence of her gaze, like she just let go of my hand.

"Thanks for having me," I say, clicking off my seat belt. "Bye."

I walk for a few seconds before looking back. The car stays put, still running. If they think our low-rise complex is bad or poor or ugly, I guess I can't tell from their faces. I just watch Siobhan climb into the front seat. They're talking. I wonder what about.

MAY

CHAPTER 17

I'm signed up to take the SAT the morning of May 4, but when I wake up, I feel like I can't breathe. I've heard other kids at school talk about panic attacks and I'm not sure if this counts. Do people just start getting these out of nowhere? Can mine be SAT-conditional? Either way, the fact that I'm freaking out over something like this—one stupid test that decides my entire future—actually makes me angry. For a second, I seriously consider rolling back over and going to sleep, just to spite the system.

Then I remember that I had to spend more than fifty bucks for this test. And that, you know, I need it to get into college. So I force myself out of bed.

I'm not expecting Mom to be up by the time I get out of the shower—there's no reason for her to be up before nine when she doesn't have work—and I'm definitely not expecting her to be sitting at the kitchen counter with a plate of French toast in front of her.

"Mom," I say, shoving my backpack out of my way. "You didn't have to do this."

I get to go into school late because of the test, so I actually have time to sit down and eat this before I go. Mom standing in front of me in a bathrobe and her hair sticking up makes me want to cry. I toss my arms around her neck and she pulls me in.

"I just wanted to send you off with some luck," she says. "You're gonna do great."

I don't know if she really believes that, but I'll take it. She sits at the counter with me and we share the plate—she drenches her bacon in syrup like a heathen and I eat the crust she won't touch. When I check my phone, there are a bunch of messages from Naomi, wishing me luck and promising we'll do something fun once we're finally free in a few hours. But there are no texts from Siobhan—weird, since I texted her last week after her mom dropped me home and a few times since then. She hasn't answered any of them.

"I hope you and Naomi have something fun planned for today," Mom says, her fork making a screeching sound against the plate. "I wouldn't want to do more school after such a big test."

"What?" I grin up at her, my phone momentarily forgotten. "Are you giving me permission to ditch?"

Mom takes a long sip from her cup, raising a brow.

"You know," she says, "back in my day, we took the SAT on a Saturday."

I'm only half listening. Naomi has texted again: *heard back yet?* I can't decide if I should text back now or just wait until we're at school to tell her that Siobhan still hasn't gotten back to me. It only makes the sickly feeling in my stomach, like I've had too much popcorn and soda before getting on a roller coaster, way worse.

I open up my texts with Siobhan. I don't *think* what I've sent her is too weird—just *thanks for the ride* and *hey how are you* and *are you ready for the test?* It's hard to tell what it means. She still says hi to me when I see her in history class, but we've all been working on our parts of the project separately, and something tells me she likes it that way.

What did I do wrong?

* * *

The test is everything I figured it would be—long and depressing and stressful. When it comes to the math section, I try my best to remember all the formulas I've been practicing, but it's hard to do that with everyone piled into an auditorium while a clock ticks loudly and reminds us about our impending doom. By the time the proctor tells us to put down our pencils, I'm pretty sure my math score is horrendous.

Other people seem to be in a similar daze as we all file out of the auditorium. There are other students in the hallway, which means it must be between periods, but I don't even care. Before I know it, I'm walking out of this building, hopefully never to return.

Until someone tugs my arm. For a quick, ridiculous second, I think it might be Siobhan. She'll be trying to catch up to me, to tell me that she lost her phone or it broke and she's sorry she hasn't had the chance to answer my texts. But it's not her—it's Naomi.

"Hey," she says. "Cody is having an afterparty at his house. Are you in?"

"Afterparty?" I try to sound surprised, but my voice is flat, like I just finished being tortured. "I don't think that's something people really do."

"Does it really matter?" Naomi shrugs. "I think we could all use a little party."

"And you could use a little Cody."

Naomi smiles, shy. I glance around the hallway again. It's pretty easy to spot who just took the SAT and who is here for a regular day of school.

"Okay, yeah," I say. "Maybe. I just don't want—"

"I doubt you-know-who will be there," she says, pulling me toward the door. "She's always volunteering at the animal shelter. Might be too busy for a party."

"It would actually be nice," I say. "If she were there."

"Why?" Naomi turns to me with raised eyebrows. "She hasn't even been answering your texts."

"Well, yeah," I say. Jesus, it really does sting when she just says it like that. "But maybe, like, she's just been busy. Or her phone is broken."

The pitying look Naomi gives me makes me feel worse than the SAT math section. She pulls out her phone with a sigh as we walk toward the student parking lot.

"Plus," I say, almost as an afterthought, "we have our presentation in APUSH on Friday. So, like, we should be communicating. We just haven't been."

Naomi sucks in a breath and rubs at her forehead. I can tell she probably wants to say a bunch of things—but instead, she just looks at me and asks, "Are you sure nothing happened that night?"

"No, I told you, we just had dinner," I say. "And her mom mentioned this girl named Erin."

"Her friend from Ireland, right?"

"Honestly, I don't know." I shrug. "Her mom said she had a crush, remember?"

"Yeah, but moms do that all the time," Naomi says with a shrug. We pause next to her car so she can fish around in her bag for her keys. "Like, remember when you thought my mom was gay because she kept calling her book club her *girlfriends*?"

"Well, yeah," I say. "But this felt different."

Naomi gives me a skeptical look before pulling her keys out.

"Even if she *did* have a crush on a girl," Naomi says, "she has a boyfriend now."

"I know."

"And she seems to really like him."

"I *know*."

Naomi bites her lip.

"Well," she says. "At least *I* love you."

I flip her off and she grins before getting in her car.

CHAPTER 18

Back in the fall, when I went to a homecoming party with Naomi, I got so drunk that I couldn't be removed from the bathroom, and she had to call my mom to lie about us having some sort of special last-minute sleepover.

I'm not going to re-create that experience this time. Mostly because I'm still a bit brain-dead from the SAT, but also because I have a mission: I'm going to figure out why Siobhan hasn't been answering my texts. Naomi listens to me talk about it on the drive, but by the time we've made it inside Cody's gigantic mansion and mingled a bit, she grabs my arm and pulls me over to a corner.

"M," she hisses, smiling tightly at a couple who walk past. "You really have to chill."

I'm holding a red cup full of soda, but I wish I'd mixed half with vodka instead. The sun is starting to go down, brilliant orange flashing into the room, and I'm trying to school my features so I don't look as pitiful as I feel. For Naomi to say this—I must be *really* bad.

"God," I say. "Am I that bad?"

Someone yells, "FUCK THE COLLEGE BOARD!" and the

living room erupts into cheers. She grins a little, shrugging one shoulder at me.

"I get it," she says. "It's a really big crush. But just . . . maybe give her some space? Talk to other people? Maybe she isn't answering for a reason."

I open my mouth, but then I see Siobhan and Danny across the room. I didn't even notice them walk in. They're standing around a group of people. Danny's arm is wrapped around Siobhan's shoulders. It looks like the group is laughing at something she just said. For a quick second, our eyes meet. I can't read her expression. Does she look embarrassed? Or am I just imagining it?

But then she turns back to Danny, laughing, and the moment is broken.

It's kind of hard to enjoy the rest of the party after that. The thing is, Naomi is almost friends with everyone—she doesn't hang out with them the way she does with me, but she makes the rounds easily, somehow knowing everyone's name and what to say to make them laugh.

I'm not really sure how to do that. I lurk in the corner while people laugh loudly at jokes I can't hear, practically falling over, and struggle to dance on rhythm at the center of the room. Whenever I spot Siobhan—dancing with a group of girls I know are on the cheerleading squad or playing beer pong with Danny and his friends—I force myself to look away immediately. I don't want to be a creep.

But it's hard. It really is. I *almost* get why Edward Cullen was such a weirdo. Not the whole "I'm gonna tell you what to do and like drive you to suicidal thoughts" part, but wanting to know everything about Bella, wanting to be around her all the time? I definitely get it. Except I don't ever want to be an Edward Cullen. And if that means trying not to look at Siobhan at all, then I guess that's what I have to do.

If I'm being honest, though, she looks really cute in her little yellow romper.

Just being honest.

By the time I end back up in the kitchen to refill my soda cup, Naomi is finally in one place, mixing herself a drink. She startles when she sees me before crushing her cup a little in her hand.

"Hey," she says, breathless. "I've been looking for you."

I raise a brow, slowly sipping from my cup.

"I've been here." I realize how bitter that sounds and clear my throat. "Were you having fun?"

Naomi nods, a little bit of her curls falling out of her ponytail.

"Definitely," she says. "I think I needed to blow off some steam, you know?"

She picks up a bunch of cups and tosses them into a nearby trash bag. I stare at her, trying my best to hide my smile.

"Dude," I say. "Why are you cleaning at someone else's party?"

"I just want to help," she says, sweeping some crumbs off the counter. "Parties can get messy."

"I can't believe you're *cleaning* for a *boy*." I shake my head in mock disgust. "Where is Cody right now, anyway?"

"Out there." Naomi nods toward the door. "Talking to his friends or something."

"And you're in here?"

Naomi bites her lip.

"Dude," I say. "Just go talk to him."

Naomi and Cody are pretty similar—both get good grades, have big houses, seem to know everyone. I never got why she hasn't just asked him out. But now, dealing with my Siobhan feelings, I get it. This shit is scary.

"He's already dealing with people," Naomi says. "It's fine."

"Okay, but you deserve a break, too," I say, gently tugging the garbage bag out of her hand. "Go dance or stare at Cody from across the room or something."

Naomi ducks her head a little. I'm about to grab her hand and drag her out to the living room myself when the door to the kitchen swings open. It's so loud I'm sure it's going to be a gigantic jock, but it's Siobhan. I can't even look away because her eyes immediately lock on mine.

"Mahalia!" It sounds like she's garbling my name. "Do you want a proper Irish tea?"

Naomi raises a brow.

"Um." Words feel like they're stuck in my throat. "No thanks, I think I'm good?"

"I'm supposed to make one for my friends," she says. "But I don't know where they went."

She turns and looks over her shoulder, but someone else walks into the room, heading straight for the liquor station. Siobhan turns back to me with a dazed smile. It's kind of terrifying. If I'm not sure how to act around normal Siobhan, I'm definitely out of my depth with a drunk Siobhan.

"Hey," Naomi says, turning toward the fridge. "Let's get you some water, huh?"

"Wait." I grab her elbow. "What happened to ogling Cody?"

Naomi glances between me and Siobhan, who leans against

the counter with her hands cupping her chin, like she's eagerly awaiting Naomi's answer.

"I can handle getting Siobhan some water," I say, lowering my voice. "Seriously."

Naomi raises a brow.

"Naomi," Siobhan says. "Who are you goggling? Googling? Ogling?"

She snorts a little. I have to bite my lip to keep from laughing. Naomi glares at me, but I can tell she's trying her best not to laugh.

"This guy in my gym class," Naomi says, heading over toward the door. "I'll tell you more when you'll actually be able to remember."

Then she's gone and it's just Siobhan and me, alone, with the sound of the party in the background. Siobhan wiggles her eyebrows at me. It's embarrassing how fast I feel my cheeks heat, even though she can't mean anything by it. I turn toward the cupboard and pull out a cup.

"Come on," she says. "You don't want a proper Irish tea?"

"I don't know." I pull the Brita out of the fridge. "What makes it proper Irish?"

"Well, first." She wags a finger at me. "You never serve tea out of the kettle. That's *wrong.*"

"Is it?"

"You serve it from a teapot," she says. *"Obviously."*

"Of course," I say, filling her cup. "And what else?"

"You add your milk," she says. "And you pour it in a cup."

"Oh." I slide the cup over to her. "That's it?"

"It's all *very* Irish," she says. "No one here does it right."

I frown. It doesn't sound like a very difficult process, but then again, I'm not exactly a tea drinker.

"*But,*" she says with a grand flourish, "I'm sure you would. If anyone could, it would be you."

Then she *boop*s me on the nose with her finger. I flinch, but she doesn't seem to notice. I'm not sure how I'm supposed to feel— she's in here complimenting me, but she's been spending all night by her boyfriend's side. Hell, she hasn't answered my texts for the last four days. I force myself to take a deep breath and push the water cup a little closer to her.

"Okay, but you need to drink your water now," I say. "Maybe you can make tea for me some other time."

She slurps loudly. Even though I shouldn't think too hard about it, I can't help but feel like her lack of response is another rejection. Jesus. I hate having a crush. It's awful.

"I have a secret."

My hands immediately start sweating.

"Uh," I say, already looking toward the door. "Maybe we can find Danny—"

"I only make tea for people I like," she says, giving me a secretive smile. "And I'd make tea for you."

"That's sweet."

"You know"—Siobhan cocks her head to the side—"I'm surprised you don't have a girlfriend."

I cough.

"You're funny, in a weird way," she says. "And you have very nice boobs. Is it because you don't like anyone at school?"

Jesus Christ. I grip the edges of the counter. Her face is flushed pink, and a few stray curls fall into her face. It's really,

really hard not to tell her how I feel right now. I know I could do it. I could tell her all about my crush, how everything feels better when she enters a room, how shitty it's been that she's been ignoring my texts. How her boobs are also very nice.

She probably wouldn't even remember it tomorrow.

But something about it feels shitty. Especially since—

"Why haven't you been answering my texts?" I try not to sound as pouty as I feel, but I don't think it works. "I thought you were mad at me or something."

Her brow furrows. She opens her mouth to say something, but then the door swings open and Danny appears. I've never been so irritated to see another person in my life.

"Babe!" He smacks a loud kiss on her cheek. "I've been looking for you everywhere!"

She turns to him, leaving me completely forgotten, with no idea how to process what just happened.

-$.20 for gas
-$150 for groceries
+$183.75 from payday
GOAL: $704

CHAPTER 19

To be honest, our history presentation on Friday is complete and utter trash.

The first sign of trouble is when we watch the first group go.

"Allow us to introduce you to . . . ," Lindsay Rocha says, projecting like she's onstage at the Democratic National Convention, "the Gulf War."

She actually does jazz hands for a few seconds. God, theater kids really do need an ego check. Celeste Schmidt nudges her, *hard,* and Lindsay stumbles a little. I'm the only one who giggles. Mr. Willis's head snaps over in my direction and he gives me a *look.* Even Danny turns his head so I can see his judgmental expression. Siobhan, on the other hand, doesn't turn around at all.

Jesus.

Despite the minor hiccup, it's easy to tell that Lindsay, Celeste, and Kevin Keegan actually rehearsed what they were going to say—and not just because of their cue cards. They finish each other's segments, easily flying through their presentation and leaving enough room for questions.

The second sign things are going to shit is what Mr. Willis

says when they've finished: "Interesting presentation. But remember, everyone, you're meant to use *three* primary sources in your presentations. Not two."

Lindsay mumbles something on her way back to her seat.

The next two groups also seem to have actually prepared. One group screens part of a documentary, while another has us analyze part of the Patriot Act. Our group was planning to mostly wing it, which suddenly seems like a catastrophically terrible idea.

I gulp.

"Well," Mr. Willis says. "Next group. Siobhan, Danny, and Mahalia will be teaching us about the infamous election of 2000."

We awkwardly shuffle to the front of the room. Siobhan stands directly in front of the SMART Board for some reason, as far away from me—and Danny—as possible. When Danny goes to stand next to her, she leans almost imperceptibly away. What the hell is going on there?

"Mahalia?" Mr. Willis gestures from his desk. "The Power-Point?"

Right. I log onto my Google Classroom from his laptop, which rests on the podium in the front of the classroom. For some reason, what I see on the computer won't appear up on the screen. Danny starts to drum against the SMART Board and it makes me sweat with irritation.

Mr. Willis seems to sense that something is wrong—maybe Siobhan was right and he just smells fear. He leans over my shoulder, studying the computer and messing around with the settings.

Five minutes isn't a long time, but it definitely feels like forever when you're standing in front of a class and your teacher is trying to figure out your PowerPoint. Danny hits a particularly jarring beat and Mr. Willis winces.

"Mr. Elliot," Mr. Willis says with a heavy sigh. "*Please* stop."

That makes me snort, just a bit, and Mr. Willis glances over at me with something that could be called a smile. Suddenly, the words *2000: STOLEN OR EARNED???* appear on the SMART Board in big black letters.

"All right," Mr. Willis says, clapping his hands together. "You're good to go."

Danny clears his throat, stepping closer to our audience, and part of me wants to beg Mr. Willis to come back. Please, please, please don't let this kid start improvising.

"So," Danny says. "You may not know that the Supreme Court had to get involved in a presidential election. In the year 2000, Al Gore and George Bush—"

"George W. Bush," I interrupt. "Not HW."

"Right," Danny says, glaring at me. "George *W.* Bush. They were running for president. But the outcome of the election would divide the country, much in the way we are divided now."

He does a grand paradiddle against the podium.

"Danny," Mr. Willis sighs.

Our classmates laugh. I roll my eyes and flip to the next slide. When I make eye contact with Siobhan, she actually holds my gaze, but I'm not sure what she's trying to communicate.

"So," I say slowly. "The electoral college . . ."

"Right," Siobhan says. Her face is paler than I've ever seen it before. "So, um, the electoral college? And slaves?"

Oh dear God. What is she even talking about? I guess I've

discovered the one thing Siobhan isn't good at. I'd laugh if my grade weren't on the line.

Danny's face has gone as red as a tomato. Mr. Willis looks extremely concerned. Siobhan coughs, then, for some reason, *keeps talking.*

"Slavery? Um." Siobhan scratches her hair. "The roots of this election . . . of the electoral college . . . were bad. Very bad. So bad it—"

"Yes, we studied how the electoral college has roots in slavery," I say, raising my voice to drown her out. "But it would play a big role in this election because of a dispute in Florida . . ."

Siobhan doubles over for a moment before shooting out of the room. Seconds later, there are gagging noises coming from the hallway. Mr. Willis runs out after her.

"EW!" Lindsay Rocha squeals. The whole class laughs.

"Jesus," I say. "Are you guys in kindergarten?"

I abandon the podium, sticking my head out into the hallway, but the scene is pretty grisly. When Siobhan croaks, "Go *away,*" I do what she says. Back in the classroom, all eyes are on me. Especially Danny's.

* * *

"I'm sorry," Naomi says. "But it sounds like she's fucking with you."

I've just finished my joke of a shift—which mostly included shadowing Bill as he did everything from checking out customers to stocking shelves—and we're walking back toward the parking lot, our aprons rumpled in our hands.

"I doubt she *pretended* to puke in the hall." I wrinkle my nose. "I don't think she could fake that."

"Not *that*," Naomi says, waving her hand. "What she pulled at Cody's party."

"I don't know," I say. "She was really drunk, right?"

"I mean, sure." Naomi presses her lips tightly together. "Anyway, I feel like maybe you could, like, focus more on getting off probation. Has Greta said anything?"

God, I get that I've been talking about Siobhan a lot, but I don't exactly want to talk about all the ways I'm failing at my job.

"No," I say, pulling my bag over my shoulder. "Am I supposed to ask her?"

"I think it's better if she tells you," Naomi says. "You don't want to seem too desperate."

If I'm being honest, though, I feel a little bit desperate. Mom used some vacation days for her recovery time, but for most of the last week, she hasn't been making any money. Between buying groceries and paying for gas, it's felt impossible to save anything.

"I still have to find a dress, too," I say, almost absentmindedly. "God, so much shit to do."

"We could try some more boutiques."

I make a face.

"Not all of them will be like the last," Naomi says. "And remember, the dress doesn't have to fit perfectly. You can always get it tailored."

I bite my lip. Getting a dress tailored to fit me seems like another expense I haven't budgeted for. Maybe there will be a cheaper solution online, like the rental space I was able to locate instead of a venue—but that's another thing I have to cross my fingers and hope to find. Why does everything in my life have to be a mess?

"Yeah," I say, running a hand through my hair. "Hey, uh, what's going on with Cody? Did you ask him out yet?"

"I already told you." Naomi's smile goes all goofy. "He's too busy with Model UN. I mean, I haven't asked him, but . . ."

I feel my phone buzz and smile at her apologetically. She knows it's probably Mom, who sometimes texts and asks me to bring things on my way home from work. But I'm shocked when I pull out my phone.

"What?" Naomi asks, seeing my face. "Did something happen to your mom?"

"No," I say. "It's Siobhan."

"Ooo," Naomi says, crowding close to my shoulder. "What does it say?"

" 'Mahalia, I'm really embarrassed about everything,' " I read out loud. " 'Can I make it up to you?' "

Naomi's eyes dart up and she wiggles her eyebrows at me.

"Come on," I say, shoving her away. "It'll probably be super awkward and weird."

Naomi purses her lips. I cock my head at her.

"I'm just . . ." Her voice trails off. "I don't know."

"You do know," I say, even as dread fills my stomach. "What are you thinking?"

"I feel like she's jerking you around a little," Naomi says. "One minute she's flirting with you and talking about your boobs—"

"Well, that's because she was drunk."

"Okay, sure," she says, crossing her arms. "But she was ignoring you for a while, right? You said she didn't even talk to you in class today. And now she wants you to come running at her beck and call?"

I shrug and shove my phone back into my pocket. She *does* have a little bit of a point. But I don't want to think of Siobhan as being manipulative. Maybe she just knows how flaky she's been and wants to make it right.

"I don't know, Naomi," I say. "You don't think that's a little harsh?"

Naomi pushes her mouth from side to side. I sigh.

"You should do what feels right," Naomi finally says. "If you want to text her, you should. Just be prepared to . . . just be friends. Or maybe not even that."

The truth is, I don't know if I can be just friends with Siobhan. I'll be too busy thinking about kissing her or holding her hand or, like, having romantic picnics with her.

"But honestly," Naomi says, "I don't know if I can handle your heartbreak for the next two weeks. "So maybe you *should* text her back."

"Excuse you," I gasp. "I listen to you talk about Cody!"

"I *barely* talk about him."

We have an intense five-second staredown before I sigh and look back down at my phone. Naomi glances over my shoulder the entire time. I'm not exactly sure what to say, so I text back, *Sure, I guess.*

"That's really convincing."

"Make up your mind, Naomi."

I want to shove the phone back in my pocket, but it beeps before I can. It's Siobhan, inviting me over to her house again. Naomi squeezes my shoulder. Something in her expression softens.

"You should go," she says. "But for you. Not for her."

"What does that even mean?"

"It *means*," she says, "the ball's in your court. If she wants to be friends again, it's your decision. If she wants to be something more, it's your decision. You can always say no. It's not all up to her. Okay?"

I know she's just trying to be realistic, but my annoying brain grabs onto the "something more" part and won't let go. Naomi says it so easily, like it's something that could really happen and not just something in my head. I guess it's real now, isn't it? *Something* is going to happen. But there's a possibility that it won't be good.

CHAPTER 20

When I pull up to Siobhan's house, there are already two cars parked in the driveway, so I park on the street instead. I hate that I'm nervous. I've never been this nervous to show up at someone's house before. Then again, it's usually just Naomi's house I show up at.

Just as I'm turning off the car, Siobhan appears in the doorway. Doodle runs alongside her as she pads toward my car in bare feet. I study her face. She's not as white as she was earlier, thank God. I don't think I can handle any more puke today.

"Hey," Siobhan says, exhaling. "I'm so glad you came."

"Yeah." I awkwardly step out of the driver's seat. "It was nice of you to invite me over."

"I was thinking we could go to the beach and then stop somewhere for something to eat."

"Are you sure about that?" I purse my lips. "Maybe we should bring a bucket with us."

"I guess I deserve that, huh?" Her faces goes red. "I'm not sick anymore. I think I just got really nervous—more nervous than I expected. But I'm sorry for ruining our project."

"You didn't ruin anything," I say, even though I'm honestly not sure if it's true or not. Mr. Willis was so busy calling custodians and the nurse that our presentation sort of fell by the wayside. "And I'm sorry, too. That was supposed to be a joke. It just wasn't very funny."

We stand there, smiling awkwardly at each other, until Doodle jumps up on my legs and I bend down to scratch her ears. I know dogs don't purr, but that's what it feels like, the way she's snuffling into my shins. Not for the first time, I wish we had a pet at home. I need more uncomplicated relationships in my life.

"I'm sorry for ambushing you the other night at the party," Siobhan says, bending down next to me. "Also, for, erm, being weird. Not answering your texts."

"Really weird," I say. Then mentally kick myself.

"Yeah." She scrunches her face up. "I didn't really mean to ignore you. Well, I—When you were over for dinner last week . . . I didn't think . . . I just talk to my mum a lot? All the time. I tell her almost everything. And I was just really upset that she would tell you something that personal."

I don't really know what to say to that. I'd probably be angry at my mom if she started talking about my crushes, too. I just don't ever tell her about them.

"That does sound embarrassing," I concede. "I feel the same way when my mom drops me off somewhere with Christian hip-hop playing in the background."

Siobhan smiles, but only a little. Doodle licks my face. Part of me wants to ask Siobhan to explain her behavior at the party—but I don't know if she even remembers. Plus, this feels awkward enough. I'm just about to make an excuse to leave when she says, "Do you want to go somewhere?"

I glance back at my car, then back at her. She's wearing a sloth T-shirt that looks like it's been washed too many times. Her hair is pulled back in a ponytail, but strands keep falling out and in her eyes. It looks like she hasn't slept properly in a few days. I can't really imagine puking in front of everyone at school. Something about it all makes my heart clench.

"Sure," I say. "Lead the way."

* * *

I think I got my dislike of sand and the beach from my mom. Neither of us has ever had a desire to sit there and do nothing all day, get our hair wet and matted, or be roasted by the sun. But it's different driving down here with the windows open and Siobhan next to me. Nicer, even if neither of us is talking.

Siobhan tells me to stop at a blue shack. There are already a bunch of people here, but none of them are from school.

"I feel like people our age never come here," she explains, sliding on a pair of flip-flops before stepping out of the car. "It's usually families and old people. No one knows what they're missing."

Inside looks like a diner from an old movie, with red booths, black-and-white tile, and a jukebox in the back corner. Siobhan slides into one of the booths without waiting for anyone to seat us, so I follow her lead and sit facing her.

"Okay, so they have the best burger in the world here," she says, pointing up at the sign for me to see. "My parents are vegetarians and our house *technically* is a meat-free zone, so you can't ever mention this—"

"Siobhan." I gasp. "Are you a secret meat-eater?"

"I know, I know." She grins. "I'm such a rebel."

I let her order for me. People around us are talking and laughing. I can't remember the last time I've been out to eat. My shoulders tense when I remember that I'll actually have to *pay* for this—more money siphoned from my party fund—but then a familiar guitar riff snaps me out of my angsty thoughts.

"Oh my God," I gush. "I *love* this song."

The thing about me is when I'm really into a song, I kind of lose my shit. It's like the part of my brain that gets embarrassed shuts down and I just let everything out.

So I'm dancing by the time the first verse has begun. And when the chorus hits, I shriek out the words—*"Tuesday, Wednesday, stay in bed / Thursday watch the walls instead"*—while banging my head like a delinquent. People turn to look at us, but I don't care. Siobhan starts out smiling and nodding along at first, but by the third chorus she's slid way down in her seat.

"Oh my God, Mahalia," she says, her face burning. "What are you doing?"

"It's FRIDAY," I yell, holding up my hands, *"I'm in LOVE!"*

"Sigh-oh-ban?" Whoever is at the counter butchers her name. "Order's up."

Siobhan practically sprints up to the counter. I continue singing and bopping around. An older lady sitting in front of me claps, smiling, and I grin back at her. Why does singing to songs you love always feel so good? It doesn't matter if your voice sucks— which mine does—as long as you feel the music. I'm so high on the song that I don't even care if I sound like a hippie. But as the song winds down, I realize Siobhan still isn't back, and I don't spot her at the counter. Did she actually *leave* me?

The song ends, and I collapse into the booth, catching my breath. I'm ready to do it all again if another bop comes on, but I don't recognize the next song. It's something that would play when a goth girl enters a scene in a teen movie from the early 2000s. I turn to look for the jukebox and find Siobhan posed dramatically in front of it, mouthing along to the words. She balances two burger baskets in one hand and grips a ketchup bottle like a microphone. I grin widely.

"Iconic," I call out. "Spectacular. Amazing."

She bows. The older lady sitting behind me whoops. By the time Siobhan is back at the table, her face is beet red, but she's also grinning.

"Wow," I say, leaning back. "I didn't think you had it in you."

"Me neither," she says. "Actually, this is something I'd never, ever do."

Siobhan slides into the booth next to me. I'm shocked for a moment but try to relax my shoulders. She's so close that I can feel her body move as she sucks in breath. This is the hardest thing about liking girls. Friends touch all the time. When I'm with Naomi, I don't think anything of the lingering touches or gazes, but it's not the same when a crush is involved. I can't tell if Siobhan means it in a flirty way or if this is just how she acts with friends.

Jesus. I need to stop. If Naomi were here, she'd remind me that I came here for answers—and I haven't gotten them yet.

"So why did you do it?" I clear my throat. "What made you sing in front of a whole restaurant?"

She turns and looks at me. Like, *really* looks at me, eyes searching my face.

"I don't know," she says. "Maybe you embolden me."

"Embolden?"

She shrugs, ducking her head, before she picks up her burger.

"Oh my God," I say, staring at it with big eyes. "You're so little. I don't know how you eat this."

She's only a few inches shorter than me, although I'm bigger around. But it's still weird to see someone so small eat something so big. She winks at me before taking a gigantic bite. She doesn't even cut it in half. I'm not hard-core enough for Siobhan.

"It's great," she says, shoving some of the food back in her mouth. "Try it."

The meat basically melts in my mouth, scalding my tongue a little, but I don't mind. It's too good for me to mind. I moan like an adult performer and Siobhan cackles. God. I could do this every day. I can't stop thinking about what she said—"you *embolden* me."

I know what Naomi said, but she's wrong. I want to kiss Siobhan. And I'm pretty sure she might want me to. I'm trying to figure out what to say when Siobhan reaches over and grabs several fries from my basket.

"I *told* you you'd like it," she says. "And now I get to live with the satisfaction of knowing that I was right and always am."

"Sure." I snort. "I haven't known you long enough to confirm or deny that."

"You'll figure it out soon," she promises. "I'm always right."

"Okay," I say, leaning back to get a good look at her. "Tell me something about myself, then."

She hums, pressing a finger against her chin.

"Well, I'm guessing you're religious. Or at least your parents are."

"Okay," I say, rolling my eyes. "But that's because my name is Mahalia. That's sort of obvious."

"I'm putting together clues!" She tries to hide a grin and fails. "It should honestly count for something. And I'm right, aren't I?"

"Sort of," I say, grabbing more fries. "My mom is super Christian. It's what gets her through the day. But I'm not. I mean, when I was younger, I definitely used to be. But I read the Bible and had a ton of questions and people got pissed at me."

"You should always be able to ask questions. That's actually kind of brave," she says. "When I had religious education to get confirmed, I just went along with everything the nuns taught us, even the things that didn't make sense to me. But it was a bit of a formality anyway."

"What do you mean?"

"I don't know. We moved around a lot and my mum is definitely, erm, different from most mothers." Siobhan shrugs. "I think it was important to her that I go, but maybe more for tradition, not the God part."

"Are they different?" I ask. My burger has disappeared before my very eyes. "Your parents, I mean. Sometimes it feels like my parents are worlds apart, and I'm not even sure how they managed to stay together long enough to have me."

She laughs and her face scrunches up again. Her burger is gone, too, so she picks up her plate and stands.

"Come on," she says. "Let's go walk on the beach."

"You didn't answer my question," I say, following behind her.

"I might not be right all the time, but I definitely can tell when people are bullshitting me, so you'd better not try it."

"Oh, Mahalia," she says, holding a hand over her heart. "I never would."

There's that flip in my stomach, even after we return our plates and start walking down to the beach. People walk past us with surfboards and boogie boards, shirtless and wearing flip-flops. It's kind of hard to focus on anything other than Siobhan.

"My parents are definitely different," she says as we walk. "I kind of wonder if that's what makes them good for each other. They balance each other out. They're from different countries and work in different places and have different-colored skin."

"And they have different ideas," I say. "I'm guessing, anyway."

"No, absolutely," she says, wrapping her arms around her stomach. "I suppose it's positive that they only argue about the stupidest things. Silly things, like what I should call them or what we should eat for breakfast, get them into a tizzy. When they have serious talks, they never seem to get upset. They've been through too much for that."

"Too much good stuff or bad stuff?"

Siobhan bites her lip, kicking some sand to the side.

"I used to want siblings when I was little," she says. "Like, really, really badly. I'd tell random people at stores that I wanted a little sibling because I thought they'd somehow be able to make it happen."

This topic change is completely out of nowhere, but I don't mind talking about this.

"Why didn't it?"

"I don't know." Siobhan shrugs. "My mum just said she was happy with me, and my dad would say they were both really busy with work. They said they wanted to give me all their attention. But when I was six, I remember my dad driving us to the hospital and he was the most emotional I'd ever seen him."

I'm silent, hands in my pockets.

"My grandmother sat with me in the waiting room, but then we went back to her house," she continues, staring straight ahead of us. "It was a little while before anyone told me there'd been a baby in my mum and that's why she was getting so tired and slow all the time. But it was gone. She was four months along."

"Oh my God," I say.

Most of the time, I don't believe in God. But still, I've grown up in church, with old Black ladies coming up to me and touching my cheeks and telling me God loves me. There's something comforting about reaching out to God, even in my head, with a prayer that's more like, "Yo, do you see me? Do you get it?" I wonder if I can extend the same comfort to Siobhan.

"God," I say again. "Fucking horrible."

There's also comfort in curse words.

"Yeah," she says, blinking hard. "I don't know. She never talks about it and I never bring it up. But I'm always reading articles about late-term miscarriages now. It must've been so fucking horrible to go through that."

"Of course," I say. "Now I feel like shit for not liking my siblings."

"You have siblings?" She turns, eyebrows raised. "You've never mentioned them."

"I mean, they're my half siblings," I say, shrugging. "And they're five and two, so it's not like there's actually anything to *talk* about. And we didn't grow up together."

"But they're little," Siobhan says. "You can't hate little kids."

"I don't *hate* them." I dig in the sand a little. "I don't know. It's like—they don't even realize what they have, you know? Both of their parents are there. It's like they have everything."

"Aw, Mahalia." She rests her head on my shoulder. I try not to tense up. "They're just babies. There's no need to be jealous."

"I know and I *hate* that I'm jealous."

"It's not their fault," she says. "But it must be hard when both of your parents aren't around. My parents weren't around a lot when I was younger because they were busy with postgrad, but I've always had cousins and aunts and grandparents."

"Yeah," I say, breathing out. "I don't have any of that. I have Naomi, but sometimes I feel weird at her house. Her parents both have these fancy jobs and they're still together and she and her siblings all get an equal amount of attention. My dad is busy with his new family and my mom is always working."

"That sounds really hard. But . . ."

I turn to face her, pausing. I already feel sand seeping into my shoes, but I don't care. It's hard not to look at Siobhan with the moon rising behind her like a movie backdrop. The planes of her face are so smooth, her skin a light brown, freckles sprinkling her cheeks. I want to kiss her. There isn't any moment when I *don't* want to kiss her. As the wind blows past us, making me wrap my arms around myself, I step closer to her.

"Just because they aren't around doesn't mean they don't love you," she says. "It just feels like it. But the things we feel aren't always fact, you know? Sometimes I feel . . ."

"Feel what?"

"It's stupid." She shrugs. "But I feel like I don't belong anywhere sometimes. People ask me questions about where I'm from or what my name means and they stare at me longer because I know they're trying to figure out what my parents look like. I don't fully belong in either one of my parents' places."

"Like where they're from?"

"Yeah, exactly," she says. "Mum isn't even from Dublin—she's from Cork, but whenever we go, it's like everyone is white. I know I'm not being oversensitive, because Dad gets it, too. But then we hang out in Oakland and I'm lighter than everyone else. I know—"

She glances at me, at my hand, darker than hers.

"I know it's not really something to complain about," she says, sighing. "But there's no one who looks like me or has parents from different countries like me. A sibling would get that."

"Someone doesn't have to get it to care," I say. "And, Siobhan—you're amazing. Seriously. It must be hard, but setting your own path . . . that's just such a cool thing you do. Maybe you've had to do that since you were little, but it's something a ton of people wish they were better at, you know?"

I pause, afraid I've said too much.

"Yeah," she says after a moment. "Everyone wants to belong, though."

"You belong with your parents," I say. "And with your family. You belong when you're with me."

Shit. Her head turns, her eyes locking on mine and refusing to let go of my gaze. Our feet are in the sand and the sun is setting. Her hair moves all over the place, blown by the wind, and her freckles stand out like constellations. Everything messy and exactly in its place.

"I think certain people are meant to be together," she says, voice lowering. "It's not really our fault if we don't meet them right away. We're just not sure until we meet the right person. Does that make sense?"

I can't breathe.

"Siobhan," I say. She asked me a question, but I can't answer it. "What you said at the party . . . did you mean—"

She leans up on her toes, presses a hand against my cheek, and kisses me. I kiss back almost like a reflex. Her lips are warm and taste like peach lip balm. What surprises me most is how natural it feels, like this is how it should be.

Until she pulls away.

Her eyes are wide, the widest I've ever seen them. I hold my hand over my mouth. My lips feel numb, the way they did when I got my first cavity and the dentist gave me Novocain. Siobhan looks a little numb, too, but not in a good way. She looks scared.

Why, though? She's the one who kissed *me*.

And I wanted it. Oh God, I wanted it. I just don't want her to regret it.

"Siobhan—"

She steps back. My heart constricts.

"I just . . ." Her voice trails off as she shakes her head. "I just need some time to figure things out."

CHAPTER 21

By the time I get home that night, I'm a tangle of different emotions.

She *kissed* me. She actually kissed me. I never imagined— She *kissed* me on the *beach* like something out of a romance novel. If she hadn't immediately freaked out, I would be certain it was all a dream.

God. As I climb up the stairs to the apartment, I can't help but feel weighed down by the way we left things—with Siobhan practically sprinting away from me. I have no idea what's going to happen next. Is she going to start ignoring me again? Is she going to tell Danny? If things were awkward before, I can only imagine how much worse they'll get if she stays with him.

When I turn my key in the lock and step inside, I'm greeted with Mom pacing the living room like some sort of nervous wreck. For a second I think I forgot to pick something up at the store—but she wouldn't have such a grim expression about me forgetting her favorite cereal.

I slowly close the door behind me. Now that she's stopped moving, I can see she's holding a Bible in her hand. God. That can't be good. A million different scenarios pass through my mind: she knows I'm gay, she knows I wasn't at Naomi's house like I told her I was, she's *pregnant*—

"Mahalia Eve," she says, lowering her glasses. "It's ten o'clock. What are you doing home so late?"

I glance at the clock above the microwave. She's right; it's ten on the dot. I just don't see what the big deal is. Other kids at school spend their Friday nights at parties that last until early in the morning. And it's not like I have a curfew, either. There's just the general understanding that Mom will kick my ass if I come home *really* late, like midnight. But ten isn't that late.

"Um, I don't know," I say. "You didn't text me, so I didn't think it was a big deal."

"I shouldn't have to text you," she says, shaking her head. "You can't just spend all your days hanging out on the streets without letting me know. Without my *permission.* If I let you spend time with your friend, I need to know you'll be back here at a decent time. Do you understand?"

Why is she freaking out about this? When I don't answer right away, she narrows her eyes.

"Yeah," I say. "Yes. I understand."

The rings under her eyes look darker than usual, which doesn't make any sense, since she was just starting to feel better. I take a step closer. The TV is on in front of us, but muted. It's playing one of the church shows she usually watches Sunday nights, except today is Friday. I glance at the table and see a bunch of envelopes, some of them from a few weeks ago, all piled on top of each other.

"Mom?" I take a seat on the couch. "What's going on?"

She takes off her glasses, rubbing her forehead. The silence seems to stretch on forever.

"I took too much time off from work," she finally says. "My boss decided to let me go."

If half of me was floating on air before the conversation, this news has tossed it to the ground with the rest of me. Hard.

"What?" I repeat. "They can't do that. Isn't that against the law?"

She cocks her head to the side, a tight smile on her face.

"Who's going to stop them, baby?"

"I don't know." I scramble through my brain. "We could report it. We could—we could find you a lawyer. They can't just *do* this."

"And where would I get the money for a lawyer?"

My mouth opens, but I don't have an answer. I doubt the money I've managed to save will pay for a lawyer. She's right. But it makes me so angry that she can be *fired* for recovering. From a job she's been at for almost five years now.

"I've thought about it all," Mom says. She sighs so heavily it seems to shake the room. "They said it was because of budget cuts, but I know it was the sick days. I was one of the first to go because I haven't worked a shift in so long. They're slick."

"But . . ." I blink back tears. "You have a kid. And bills to pay. Do they even care?"

"Mahalia." Mom rubs her forehead. "Sometimes . . . these things happen."

"Yeah, well."

I *want* to say that "these things" are bullshit, but she's not too sick to wash my mouth out with soap, like she did when I was thirteen and discovered the word *fuck*.

"We're going to have to start cutting corners, baby," Mom continues. "I'm trying to figure things out. But it looks like I won't be able to match the money for your party. I'm sorry."

I literally start crying at that moment. It's the most embarrassing, bratty thing I've ever done, but I immediately burst into tears. Mom looks like she feels even worse.

"Are you sure?" I say. "It's really that serious?"

But it's a stupid thing to say, a stupid thing to ask, and I'm sure we both know it. I've already been paying for groceries and gas. If there was any money squirreled away, she probably already used it. I *know* it's not her fault. But I'm still sad—and angry and upset.

We never get to have nice things. Something always interferes at the last minute. Last year, an overdue rent bill and lack of savings meant I couldn't have a Sweet Sixteen. When I was thirteen, my younger sister being born meant Dad couldn't show up to my final choir concert of the year. The summer after eighth grade, I couldn't go to a music camp I found online because it was too expensive and they didn't offer scholarships. When the girl I like finally kisses me, there's a problem, something wrong.

Every single time I want something, even if it's small, if it seems possible, it gets taken away. It's like I can't have anything at all.

"I'm sure, baby," she says. "I'm really sorry."

I cover my eyes with my face.

"This fucking *sucks*."

"Language," she says, like I knew she would. "I know this is hard, but—"

"I wish you hadn't promised me." My voice is muffled by my hands. "I never would've gotten my hopes up if you hadn't promised."

I can't see her expression, but her silence tells me how she feels.

"I said I'd *try* to match the money," she says after a long moment. "I never promised."

My throat feels raw, like I just swallowed something sharp. I wipe roughly at my face and nod at the ground. It's fine. It's okay. I'm still going to make my party happen—I have most of the money for the deposit ready, and once I'm off probation, it won't take me long to raise the rest.

And Mom? She's going to be fine. We've had money issues before. She's going to find another job. It's going to happen. All of this is going to be fine.

So why is my entire body drooping, like I'm already anticipating more disappointment?

"You're right," I say, pushing myself out of my seat.

Then I turn and walk into my room. She doesn't follow.

CHAPTER 22

My dad once told me that falling in love with a woman is like holding your breath. I always thought he was being incredibly dramatic and annoying, but now I understand. I spend all weekend in bed, miserable, and you'd think the reason would be Mom losing her job. But it's Siobhan I can't stop thinking about—the way she grabbed my face in her hands, the way she pulled me in like she just couldn't help herself. Maybe I need this to distract me from the whole Mom situation.

I keep rethinking all our interactions. How does she feel right now? What is she thinking about the kiss? Why won't she answer my messages? I want to text and ask if she needs time, but that feels stupid and presumptuous. The worst part is that I *wanted* that kiss. I really, really wanted it. But I'm not sure if I'd trade one kiss for the price of never speaking to her again.

"Give that back to me," Naomi says. "Greta has eyes everywhere."

I blink back to Earth. My probation has been lifted now, so I'm free to stock boxes of pasta with Naomi without Bill's watchful scanning for mistakes, but I'm still on reduced hours and lower pay.

"I can't believe this," Naomi says, smacking her palms against her apron. "You're so far gone. It's kind of scary, actually."

"It's so annoying." I rub my hands over my eyes. "I wish I could make it stop."

"No, you don't."

"I do."

"You'd want to stop liking her? And for her to stop liking you?"

"I don't even *know* if she likes me."

"Mahalia." Naomi grabs my hands and moves them away from my face. "She kissed you. Let's be rational here, all right? We're pretty sure she likes you. We're pretty sure she has a boyfriend she likes. We're pretty sure she kissed you while they were still together."

"I didn't mean for it to happen," I say. "It just did."

"You sound like everyone in the middle of every affair ever."

"It's not an *affair.*"

She gives me a pitying look and I don't even feel bad about it.

"Maybe I'll write her a letter."

"A letter?" All goodwill immediately flies off Naomi's expression. "Mahalia . . ."

"What?"

"No one even reads letters anymore," she says, shaking her head. "It'll make you look like a lovesick old man."

"That's what makes it *romantic.*"

The joke doesn't really land. Naomi just rolls her eyes and turns back to the pasta shelf. But there must be something telling about my silence because she turns to me after a moment, softening her voice as she asks, "How are things going with your mom?"

God, the absolute last thing I want to talk about.

"It's fine," I say. "You know, I'm still going to save for my party and everything. It's going to be fine."

The truth is that Mom and I avoided each other all weekend. Mom has been pretty busy with her computer, probably looking up jobs. If I'm honest, though, I probably wouldn't want to talk to her even *if* we hadn't had our little tussle. There's nothing I can do to help her find a job, and I'd rather not let slip any details about Siobhan.

"Are you sure?"

"What do you mean, am I sure?" I say. "Jesus, Naomi."

"Sorry, sorry," Naomi says, holding up her hands. "I didn't mean that."

I want to say something, but I'm interrupted by a sob. Naomi's eyebrows shoot up. I tiptoe out of the aisle and Naomi follows behind me. There's an older man, in a suit, crying over the avocados.

"Oh no," Naomi whispers. "Do you think there's something wrong with him?"

"I don't think anyone cries like that over avocados."

We stare at him for a second. He pulls a handkerchief out of his coat pocket and wipes at his face. Oh God. I hate watching other people cry. It's even worse when *adults* cry. My mom has always made a habit of crying when she doesn't think I'm around, but I've definitely heard her before. I never know what to do then and I don't know what to do now. It just makes me want to walk far away.

But Naomi grips my wrist, pulling me forward. I don't even get the chance to ask if we're doing the right thing—if maybe this guy *wants* to cry in front of avocados without anyone watching—before we're standing in front of him.

He looks even sadder up close. The skin around his eyes is pink and there are wrinkles on his face. The fact that something bad, like *really* bad, could've happened makes me feel sick.

"Hello, sir," Naomi says. She sounds like she's talking to a small animal. "I'm Naomi and this is my friend Mahalia. We saw you over here and thought you could use some help."

"Yeah," I say. "Are the avocados really that bad?"

Naomi glares at me.

He ducks his head a little before glancing between the two of us, dabbing at his eyes with the pocket hanky a little more. Something about the motion makes him seem even sadder. He's holding a basket, but there are only a few boxes of graham crackers in it.

"Oh no," he says, tucking the square back into his pocket. "I'm so sorry. I didn't think there was anyone here. There's nothing wrong with the avocados. They're perfect. The produce here is always perfect."

Somehow, Naomi appears to be lost for words. I want to touch him, put a hand on his shoulder or something, but I'm not sure how to do it without being awkward, especially since he keeps turning away like he's embarrassed.

"Don't worry," I say. "It's just us, and Naomi's the only one who really does any work. I just hide and try to avoid all of my responsibilities."

She glares at me again, but to my surprise, the man chuckles.

"That's funny," he says. "Maybe that's why I haven't seen you around."

"We have school, too," Naomi says. "So that's part of it."

"Yes," the man says, nodding. "That could also be it."

"Can we help you find anything?" I glance at his basket. "Like, other than graham crackers? No offense, but that brand sucks."

Naomi nudges me. Maybe that wasn't the right thing to say, either.

"Oh," he says, glancing down at the boxes. "No, no thank you. These used to be my daughter's favorite."

"Did she move on to a superior snack food?"

"No," he says. "She passed away."

Shit. I definitely need to stop talking. Naomi gives me her *are you kidding me* look.

"I'm sorry," I say at the same time Naomi says, "I'm so sorry for your loss."

"Thank you, girls," he says, sniffling. "It's been two years, but you have to understand, this isn't something you ever get used to."

No one in my life has ever died. All I can think about is this one time in preschool, when we read a book where a kid grew up and his mother died. I was inconsolable. I didn't realize *my* mom would die one day. I still can't even imagine it. What would I do without my mom? What does *anyone* do without their mom? It must be even worse when you lose a kid.

"I'm sorry," I say again. "The graham crackers aren't so bad."

"Oh no," the man says, chest rising in laughter. "They're horrible. They taste like sawdust."

"Yes," I say, probably a little too loud. "Exactly! I keep saying that and everyone just gives me weird looks."

I get that everything in the store is supposed to be organic. It's Greta's *brand* or something. But that doesn't mean everything has to taste horrible.

"Thank you, girls," he says. The smile he gives is small, a bit forced, but it's something. "I needed a laugh."

I think I did, too. That doesn't keep Naomi from nudging me in the ribs when he walks away.

"Mahalia, what's *wrong* with you?" she snaps. "What if he started crying again?"

"Well. He didn't. So."

"Ugh," she says. "I can't deal with you."

"You love me."

"Yeah," she says, walking back to the pasta aisle. "Whatever."

But I still haven't heard back from Siobhan. And my heart aches, just a little.

CHAPTER 23

Mom has asked me for things before. She's wanted me to wash the dishes, send thank-you notes to my grandparents, pay for gas. But I'm kind of shocked that she'd ask me for this.

"I know it's a lot," Mom says, rubbing her forehead again. "I know. But I'll give it back to you."

It's Tuesday and I'm literally already late for school, but she asked me right before I ran out the door, and I'm pretty sure she planned it that way. I dig my teeth into my lip.

"When do you need it by?"

Mom doesn't look at me. She spreads her hands on the table.

"The electric is already late," she admits. "I've been trying to—I'm not asking for the whole thing. Just for a hundred dollars."

I hate everything about this—Mom not looking at me, her back hunched like she's begging, the fact that she's asking *me* for money. Who else did she ask before she had to ask me? I know my grandparents have refused to give her money ever since she got pregnant with me, and my dad always *says* he'll help. For a second, I have to wonder if she already asked him and then came to me in a last-ditch effort.

I know it's a fucking asshole thought, but I can't help but think that she already technically *owes* me. And that I shouldn't feel a lump in my throat over this.

"You know what?" Mom pushes the pile of bills away from her. "Actually, never mind. Don't worry. Head to school. I'll figure it out."

I pull my phone halfway out of my pocket. I'm only getting later. My homeroom teacher, Mrs. Tell, is going to kill me. When I glance up, Mom's throat is bobbing as she looks down at an envelope. There are so many crossed-out numbers on the back that it makes my eyes cross.

"It's fine," I say, stepping back toward the door. "The money is in the blue shoe box under the bed—you can grab it from there."

Mom glances up. I can't look at her expression for long—the mix of hope and embarrassment is too much.

"Are you sure?"

"Definitely." I nod, already halfway out the door. "It's not a problem."

I don't mean to slam the door behind me, but I do. And then I spend the entire ride to school struggling not to yell out on the highway.

* * *

I'm at lunch with Naomi when I get the text.

Meet me at the beach tonight. Please, please, please. I really need to talk to you.

I have to read it three times before it fully sinks in. Even then, I'm not happy, not the way I should be. I've wanted to scream since I walked into school this morning, and Siobhan's text definitely isn't making the feeling go away. I can barely eat the lunch Naomi brought me from her house—and she always brings the best shit, gourmet kettle chips and cheeses with names I can't pronounce.

"Mahalia?" Naomi says, putting down her sandwich. "Is it your mom?"

"No," I say, super fast, shoving a potato chip into my mouth. "No, it's not that. Look at this."

Naomi squints at the text.

"Oh," she says. "This is good, right?"

"I don't know," I say. "What if it's, like, bad news?"

Siobhan could tell me she doesn't want to hang out anymore. And honestly, maybe that would be for the best. Maybe I wouldn't be so torn up about her all the time. But hearing her say that—it's going to be hell.

"I mean . . ." Naomi purses her lips. "She probably wants to talk about boundaries."

I toss back my head and groan so loud that it's almost a yell. No one looks over amid the chaos of the school cafeteria.

"Seriously," Naomi says, chomping on some kettle chips. "It doesn't sound bad."

"She has a boyfriend."

"Mahalia," Naomi says. "Just hear her out."

"I guess."

For the rest of the day, the text is all I can think about, even at work. But I also have to actually try to do my job well. I can't afford to be on probation again. When I complain about it to

Naomi, she squirts some of the fruit in the produce aisle with her water bottle.

"Welcome to the real world," she says grandly. "My parents are always talking about bills and how we should learn the value of a dollar and everything."

"But it's different for you guys."

"What do you mean?" She raises a brow. "We have bills just like you."

"Oh, come on," I say, stepping away from her so I can spray the cucumbers. "There's a difference between bills for three kids in a big house and a bunch of cars and the crappy one-bedroom apartment that my mom and I are struggling to pay for."

She's silent for a long moment. I close my eyes, silently cursing myself. Why would I say that? Part of me wants to take it back, but the other part says screw it. It's not like I actually *did* anything. I just told the truth.

The only sound is the loud, off-key strings of some endless Michael Franti song playing on the loudspeaker. I glance over to see that Naomi is holding her water bottle close to her chest. I sigh and step closer.

"Listen, Naomi—"

"Hello, girls."

I turn my head. It's the same guy who was crying in front of the avocados yesterday. He's wearing a suit—or what looks like one anyway—except without the jacket. This time, thankfully, he's not crying. He's actually smiling. The one time we're fighting, this dude comes to see us. Very deliberately, he holds out an avocado. I can't help but smile.

"Oh," Naomi says. "Hi, Mr. . . ."

"Oh, just call me Jimmy," he says, waving his hand. "I already know your names. I wasn't sure when you'd be working, but I didn't think I'd find you so fast."

"Well, you know me," Naomi says. "Always working. Not Mahalia, though."

I would normally laugh. Now it feels like a jab.

"Right," he says. "I remember."

It doesn't take her long to check out the single avocado and toss it in a bag for him. But even after she passes him his receipt, he lingers.

"Is there anything else we can do for you?" I ask. "Do you need help finding something else?"

"No, no." His face sobers for a second. "I just wanted to thank you again."

"We really didn't do anything," Naomi says. I nod.

"It felt like something to me," he says, a tentative smile appearing. "I wanted to thank you for that. If there's ever a way I can return the favor, let me know."

I think the reason why white guys, even old ones, can get whatever they want is because we're all programmed by society to want to take care of them. I shouldn't care about how some random white dude in the supermarket feels, and yet here I am, almost choked up over his quiet words.

"Oh," I say. "We couldn't take anything from you."

"Well," he says. "I'll just visit every now and again. It was nice seeing you girls. Till next time."

He walks off before we can say anything. I turn to say something to Naomi, but she's just gone back to squirting the produce.

God. This is definitely going to be a long day. I sigh and go back to my own water bottle.

* * *

Siobhan is waiting for me near the entrance to the beach when I pull up. That means I can't even run away to hide. Shit. I park the car and rub my sweaty hands on my shorts. I wonder how this is going to work—will she take her time or rip off the Band-Aid? When I get closer, I see that her hair is tied back into a short pony-tail and she's wearing another pair of overalls. She actually looks nervous. Something tugs at my heart.

"Hey," she says, all soft. "I'm glad you came."

"Yeah."

She glances behind us, like someone is watching, before holding out her hand. I blink down at it. She slaps it against her side.

"Okay," she says, clearing her throat. "Can we walk a little bit?"

I bite my lip and nod, not trusting myself to speak. I walk next to her, trying to leave enough distance that we're not on top of each other, but I also don't let her get too far. I'm trying my best to think of something to say when she finally starts talking again.

"I'm sorry," she says. "For—for running away. That wasn't cool."

I almost trip over my own feet.

"I know things are confusing for you," I say, shoving my hands in my pockets. "But I wish you would've just . . . *talked* to me."

"I know," she says. The corners of her mouth twitch. "I'm sorry for taking another whole weekend to talk to you again."

I glare at her out of the corner of my eye. Her smile vanishes.

"Okay," I say, turning my entire body toward her. "Why'd you even drag me out here?"

I can already picture it. She'll say she's never kissed a girl before, that she's always wanted to. That she's still with Danny and isn't going to break up with him. That she still wants to be friends. I'm pretty sure the whole conversation will kill me.

"I don't know," she says, and there's the nervous flicker in her eyes again. "I mean . . ."

"What is it?" I press.

"Ugh." She tosses her head back. "Mahalia, I'm—I've never been in this situation before. I promise that I'm—I've thought about this so much. Every moment since it happened. I haven't been able to stop."

My throat goes dry. I want her to stop and I also want her to keep going.

"It's—I've never—I'm not doing this the way I wanted to." She grabs at some of her hair. I want to grab her hand, but my entire body is frozen. "I've—I've had crushes on girls before. I think. I've just never—it sounds cliché, but I thought it was a phase. And I never had a girlfriend. I've never dated a girl. Do you understand what I'm saying?"

She barely pauses long enough for me to register it.

"And still, I . . ." She shakes her head. "Everything is different here. Maybe it would be simpler, if it weren't for Danny. That's what I've been thinking about. Once you and I started spending more time together, being with you felt so easy, and I found myself looking forward to it, even when I was with him. And it made me feel so horrible."

She takes a deep breath, closes her eyes. "It still makes me feel horrible."

"It's okay," I hear myself saying. "Really. I get it."

Her eyes snap open. "You do?"

"Yeah." My voice cracks. I clear my throat. "Look, I get it. I mean . . . he's your boyfriend. And the kiss was just a spur-of-the-moment thing. So I get if you—"

"No," she says. "I don't think you do. Mahalia, I broke up with Danny this morning."

My eyes widen. Siobhan's looking at me with this intense gaze, like she's willing me to understand. But I . . . Could this really be happening? This entire time, I was gearing myself up for her rejection, but . . .

"Are you serious?"

"I know," she says. "I know. It's a lot. But I—I like you. This—spending time with you—*kissing* you—it means a lot to me. I'd like to keep doing it."

I open my mouth, but nothing comes out. She holds her hands together. It's like she's a little kid begging me to get her a doll for Christmas. But this isn't some doll I can't afford. She's telling me she *likes* me, the same way I like her.

"Oh shit," I say. "I like you, too. Like, I *really* do."

Then I kiss her, hard.

I feel like I could fly.

Second Draft of a Playlist for Siobhan

(with input from Naomi)

* "Isn't She Lovely" by Stevie Wonder
  This is about a baby. Mahalia. Stop.
  I just wanted to see if it would work!
  Well, it doesn't.

* "Every Breath You Take" by the Police
  This song is creepy.
  I mean, yeah, but most people don't listen to the lyrics too closely, so it kind of ends up being romantic.
  What if she listens to what he's saying????
  What if she just listens to the sound of his voice?
  Mahalia, you're going to freak her out. I'd run away.

* "Love My Way" by the Psychedelic Furs
  Is this a love song?
  I don't know. I guess it could be?
  I thought the whole point was to add love songs, though?

* "Lose My Breath" by Destiny's Child
  APPROVED

* "Please, Please, Please, Let Me Get What I Want" by the Smiths
  Girl. This is just kind of pathetic.

* "Mercy Mercy Me (The Ecology)" by Marvin Gaye
  A song about the environment???
  Well, yeah, but it can have an alternate meaning. Like how I look at her and think "Mercy Mercy Me"?
  . . . that's weird.

* "Whatta Man" by Salt-N-Pepa
  Can I still use this even though she's not a man?
  Uh, I think?

* "Burnin' Up" by the Jonas Brothers

  Naomi. No way.

  I'm pretty sure this is a classic.

  Go away.

* "When a Man Loves a Woman" by Percy Sledge

  Again, does this work for a girl?

  Uhhhh, maybe? But I'm pretty sure my parents danced to this at their wedding, so it might be a lot.

* "Crazy in Love" by Beyoncé

  I don't really want Jay-Z anywhere on this playlist.

  Ugh, are you always going to be mad?

  Yes!!!!!!

* "Brown Eyed Girl" by Van Morrison

* "My Girl" by the Temptations

  Too soon.

  For real?

  Definitely.

* "Happy Together" by the Turtles

  This song sounds kinda sinister.

  I think it's cool???

  Okay, let's see what Siobhan says.

* "Can't Take My Eyes Off You" by Frankie Valli and the Four Seasons

  You should try to find Heath Ledger's version.

* "I'll Make Love to You" by Boyz II Men

  Not only is this SUPER weird because you are not having sex yet and might not ever get to that point, but you're starting to sound like my dad right now.

  It's romantic!

  . . . if my dad agrees with you, there's a problem.

CHAPTER 24

On Thursday, I'm not paying attention when Mr. Lewis, my English teacher, walks past and places the test on my desk. It's face-down, so I have to flip it over to see the grade. Sixty-eight. I kiss my teeth.

Mr. Lewis walks back to the front of the class. It feels like he's staring right at me when he says, "For some of you, this test wasn't your best. I'll be around after class if you'd like to discuss your grade. Now, on to *The Catcher in the Rye* . . ."

Across the room, Naomi catches my eye for a quick moment, but I look back down at my desk. I *should* be stewing over the fact that I got such a low grade when English is usually pretty easy for me. My head was somewhere else when I took the test—caught between Siobhan and Mom's mounting bills.

"It's interesting how rich Holden is," Lindsay Rocha says. "I think it influences the way he views New York."

"Yeah," another girl, Alison Richards, says. "Like in his normal life, when he isn't at school, he probably goes to fancy black-tie parties at the Plaza all the time."

The discussion continues, but I start doodling. Usually that's something I reserve for math or science classes. But lately, my head has felt all foggy whenever I'm in *any* class, and doodling helps.

Before I realize what I'm doing, I've sketched out a dress—the type *I'd* wear if I went to a black-tie party at the Plaza. I lean back in my seat and take a good look at it. The dress is off-the-shoulder, with six tiers made of chiffon that reach all the way down to the floor in soft pleats. If I had colored pencils, I'd sketch out the rainbow colors I see in my head.

After going to that nightmare boutique with Naomi, I thought I'd lost my taste for fancy dresses. But this one is perfect. I can see myself flouncing into the party, all eyes on me, the fabric swishing magically against my legs. I can see it.

Suddenly, something flies in front of my face. I jerk back, almost falling out of my seat, only to see that it's just a football. Who the hell is throwing a football around a classroom in *May*?

"Mr. Elliot," Mr. Lewis snaps. "Would you like to visit the office?"

Danny is sitting in one of the back rows, grinning stupidly, because of course he is.

"No," he says. "Sorry."

The bell rings, but it does nothing to stop the giggles.

"Don't apologize to me," Mr. Lewis says. "Apologize to Ms. Harris."

God. I don't want Danny to apologize to me. I don't even want him to talk to me, especially after our disaster of a presentation. I pack up my books as fast as I can, but it doesn't keep Danny from lumbering toward me. His football has rolled over by the window.

"Sorry," he says in a flat tone. He doesn't even make eye contact with me.

"Yeah," I say. "Whatever."

He wastes no time jogging over to his friends in the hallway. God. I hate Danny. I shove my books into my bag and head for the door, but Mr. Lewis holds out a hand when I pass his desk.

"Mahalia," he says. "Do you think you could stay a minute? I'll write you a pass."

Shit. I hold back a sigh. Mr. Lewis isn't one of those *cool* teachers who tries to rap about history or shows movies every week, but I know he cares. I sort of wish he didn't. Then maybe I could get through these next few months in peace.

The last student walks out, glancing at me like they're sad they won't get to witness the drama, and I step up to Mr. Lewis's desk. It's littered with different books and papers. A picture of his family is in the corner. He clears his throat and I look up at his face.

"I'm fine," I say. "It was just a football."

"Oh—that," Mr. Lewis says. "Well, I'm glad you're all right. But that's not what I wanted to talk about."

I swallow. Did he notice me doodling?

"Mahalia," he says. "We know this last test wasn't your best."

"Yeah," I say, pulling at my backpack strap. "Sorry. It's been a rough few weeks."

He nods, staring at me. I'm not sure what I'm supposed to do. Maybe he's expecting me to launch into a speech about all my problems, but this isn't a teen drama or an episode of *Boy Meets World*.

Eventually, he clears his throat, leaning forward.

"Mahalia," he says again. "You're one of my best students. But now, between this test and some recent homework assignments you've missed, I'm worried about you."

"I mean, my mom had surgery a few weeks ago," I say. "And I have my job. So I just—it's all been a lot. But I'll be better. I promise."

I regret the words as soon as they're out of my mouth. His expression has changed. I know this isn't about me slacking off anymore. He's probably thinking I'm a poor Black girl. Like I'm a character from *The Blind Side*. I wish I'd never mentioned anything about my home life.

"Do you have a place to do homework at home?" he asks. "The library is open until four—"

"No, I do," I say. "I do. It's just been an adjustment. But I'm fine. Really."

He eyes me again for too long of a moment. I'm praying he doesn't say anything else that jabs at my pride.

"Well," he says, flipping over a notebook. "I'm going to need you to stay after school."

"What?" My eyebrows shoot up. "Why?"

"Like I said, I'm worried." He glances up at me, his expression serious. "I think it would be a good idea for you to carve out some time to focus on your schoolwork."

"But—"

"Mahalia." He folds his fingers together. "It's junior year. You know how important it is."

I shove my hands into my pockets. I could argue, but he's right. It's embarrassing that my teacher even has to talk to me about my grades.

"Today, after school," he says, writing my name in the notebook. "You can take the late bus home."

I probably *could* stay after, since my shift doesn't start until three. But I simply don't want to.

"Are you sure—"

"Mahalia," he says. "This is your future we're talking about."

I stare down at the pass in his hand. Part of me wants to ask if this is a punishment, some sort of detention, but I already know the answer. I take the pass out of his hands and leave.

* * *

It turns out that I'm not the only poor soul stuck with Mr. Lewis after school. I only recognize one of the three other kids, and no one talks to anybody else. I can't help but notice that two of them are brown and one is Black. We sit in silence working on homework while Mr. Lewis walks around the room, leaning over to offer advice here and there. There's something about his tone that makes my skin crawl—like he gets off on swooping in and playing savior.

"By the way," Mr. Lewis says, passing by my desk. "My door is always open if you need help with college essays. Maybe there's a compelling story to pull out of your . . . recent *struggles*. A silver lining, if you will."

What? I glance at the other students, but not one of them looks up, as if they've heard this same spiel before.

I click my pen a few times, feeling a hot wave of shame that my current essay draft is just as stereotypical as what he's suggesting. It's about being the first person in my family to go to college after my parents had me as teens. The thought of sharing it with Mr. Lewis makes my stomach turn.

"Um, Mr. Lewis?"

My head immediately snaps toward the door. I'd know her voice anywhere—it's Siobhan. I can't stop the corners of my mouth from turning up at the sight of her. We haven't spoken for a few days, not even today in history class, where Danny refused to look at her even once. What's she doing here?

Mr. Lewis walks toward her. "Yes?"

"Um, Mrs. Herbst needs Mahalia's help with something," she says, not looking over at me. "She's putting together the school newspaper and needs to fix a quote from Mahalia."

Mr. Lewis glances back at me. I duck my head, digging into my copy of *Catcher*.

"Are you sure you can't just do it here?" he asks. "She's in the middle of—"

"We're doing the design right now," Siobhan says. "So we actually really need her. The other student, uh, they—they lost their thumb?"

It comes out like a question. I close my eyes, forcing myself not to laugh.

"Their thumb," Mr. Lewis repeats. "*How?* And what does that have to do with—"

"It was a freak accident," Siobhan says, her words practically jumping over each other. "She—it—got caught. In an elevator. And now . . . we can't interview her because she's in the hospital."

Mr. Lewis glances back at me again, but I refuse to look up. I might burst into laughter.

"Also," Siobhan adds, "the story is about slavery. So we can only ask Black students."

Mr. Lewis looks like he's having a stroke.

"It's very important," Siobhan says, folding her hands together, "that we talk about important parts of the country's history and how racism—"

"All right," Mr. Lewis says, shaking his head over and over. "Just take her."

Siobhan grins at me as I bolt out of my seat. She grips my arm, the two of us practically skipping down the hallway, giggling to each other.

"Siobhan," I say. "What the *fuck* was that?"

Her face is red and she can't stop laughing. I want to kiss her.

"I've noticed Americans get uncomfortable when you mention slavery," she says, shrugging a little. "And—well, I panicked."

"Thank God you didn't puke again."

"That was *one* time . . ."

CHAPTER 25

"Wait, so what's the actual point of hiking?"

Somehow, between us sneaking out of the school building and Siobhan directing me while I sped out of the parking lot, we ended up here. Hiking. Instead of, you know, doing anything involving kissing.

"Well, hiking makes me happy and helps us connect to nature—"

I let out a loud groan.

"*And*," she adds, nudging me, "I *did* save you from detention."

I can't help but grin a little, even as I say, "It wasn't detention."

"Oh?"

I pause, doubling over. Sweat is practically pouring out of me. Siobhan is, evidently, the type of person who carries around hiking boots in her car. I borrowed a pair of hers, but they feel awkward on me, like they're weighing me down. Siobhan isn't sweating at all. She's actually glowing. I, on the other hand, am absolutely dripping. And, according to Siobhan, this isn't even a *real* hike. She took me to the shortest hiking trail she could find.

"No," I say, straightening. "Just a mandatory after-school study session."

"Oh, if it was only *that*—"

I kiss her quick, at the corner of her mouth, and savor the way her eyes crinkle. Kissing her on the mouth when I haven't asked her about it first still feels weird. Even though we've spent time together before, it feels like I'm still learning so much about her.

She laughs but places a hand on my back, between my shoulder blades. We're close enough that I'm pretty sure I'm dripping sweat on her. I move to step away, but she pulls me closer.

"I'm pretty sure," I say in between breaths, "that my long-lost asthma has returned from war."

"You're still passing enough air to make sarcastic comments," she says, slapping my back. "And look, we made it to the top. Look at how beautiful it is."

If she were anyone else, I'd roll my eyes. But, really, I'm kind of in love with her and the dopey face she makes when she looks over the edge of the cliff. It's not a real cliff, like the one Bella jumps off in the third *Twilight* movie. There's a bunch of dirt and grass around us. Over the edge, there's a sparkling coastline hugged by gigantic trees. Everything is green—it's an image that belongs in a storybook. I guess she really *does* have a point.

"It's pretty," I admit, standing back up. "But, like, you're prettier."

"Mahalia." She glares at me, the corners of her mouth twitching. "You're *so* bad at flirting."

"Well, it wasn't flirting. It was a compliment."

"You're bad at those, too."

"Damn, tough crowd." I shake my head. "Sorry, not my best material. I'm too busy dying of heatstroke over here."

"Aw, poor baby." She nudges my shoulder. "Do you want me to kiss it better?"

I kiss her first. Even though I'm sweaty, her hands are on my hips, and I put mine on her face. Her cheeks are just as soft as her lips.

I guess I'm kind of in love with hiking, too.

Later, after we've managed to climb back down to a less dizzying altitude, we grab Italian ices from this place a few blocks from Siobhan's house. Sitting in the car with her, sharing flavors and giggling at nothing . . . I can't remember the last time I was this happy.

Then Siobhan breaks the silence. "How did you know you were gay?"

I startle a little but still manage to swipe a spoonful of bubble gum ice from her cup.

"It took a little while, I think." I suck the syrup out of the ice. "My mom used to send me to church camp every year, right?"

"Like a camp in the woods?"

"No, more like we went to the local church all day," I say, pursing my lips as she laughs. "It was actually kind of fun. We played games and had snacks. But there was one girl in my group named Isabel. As the legend goes—"

"The legend?"

I stick my tongue out at her. She doesn't laugh, though, and leans forward instead.

"How does the legend go?"

"We played Truth or Dare one day, and someone dared someone else to kiss a girl," I say. "I don't remember who it was, just that no one would do it. And I didn't think it was a big deal—neither did Isabel, because I kissed her, and she kissed me back."

Naomi usually laughs or rolls her eyes when I tell this story. Siobhan just nods slowly.

"And that was it?" she asks. "That's when you knew?"

"It was a little more complicated." I stick my spoon in my ice. "We kept kissing that summer, whenever we were alone, but we were scared we'd get caught. And I still liked boys. It was confusing."

"Yeah." She nods, slow. "I think I . . . I think I still like boys."

"It's fine."

It's more than fine. Everything is perfect. I feel like jumping on top of the roof of my car and dancing all around. Nothing could change the way I feel right now.

"Seriously. I don't even know if I'm bisexual anymore," I say. "I was talking to Cal, you know, Naomi's little sibling? And we were talking about being pansexual. So maybe that's me."

I'm expecting her to ask what that means, but she just nods, ditching her spoon and holding the plastic cup to her mouth to lick at the ice instead. Her tongue is pink. Maybe I shouldn't look at her tongue. This is all so new that I'm not sure what the rules are.

"I read about it," she says, blushing a little. "We have pansexuality in Ireland, too, you know."

I nod, spooning more cherry ice into my mouth. This is actually the best day ever. I don't mind being close to the beach, not when I'm with her. Now that we've talked this through, we can hang out without things being weird. I still don't know *exactly* what I'm doing. It's not like I've ever had a girlfriend before.

But I don't feel scared. I don't feel like I'm going to mess everything up.

I feel kind of hopeful.

"So what does this mean?" I ask, plopping my spoon in my empty cup. "For the two of us, I mean. Are we . . ."

"Girlfriends?"

A wisp of hair has fallen out of her ponytail. I brush it out of her face, my thumb lingering on her cheek. She stares down at my hand and back up at my face for a moment. I can't tell what she's thinking. I wonder how long it'll take for me to learn her expressions, what the furrowing of an eyebrow means, if she purses her lips when she gets mad. Siobhan runs a finger over the back of my hand, slowly turning it over. She's staring right into my eyes when she kisses my palm. My stomach grows hot.

"Sure." My voice sounds high, even to my ears. "Girlfriends. If that's what you want, I mean."

She leans forward, so close that I can feel her breath against my lips. So close that I can barely see her whole face. My eyes are like a camera going out of focus.

I always thought my own brown eyes were plain and boring, but Siobhan's are beautiful. They're so deep I feel like I could get lost in them, like the dreams where I'm falling, with no end in sight. The only difference is that now I *want* to fall.

"Of course it's what I want," she says. "Of course it is."

This time, we move in for the kiss simultaneously. It's even better than before.

−$150 for groceries

GOAL: $1,408

CHAPTER 26

I'm down bad.

Being around Siobhan makes it easy to forget everything—how I'm waiting for my SAT score, writing my college essay, and the fact that I'm hundreds of dollars away from my goal and getting further by the day. But when I have to come back down to Earth? That shit hits me hard.

At work on Thursday, I throw myself so hard into being a model employee and Greta actually notices.

"Mahalia," she says, placing her hands on my shoulders. "I'm proud of how far you've come."

Greta has a little chart outside her office with all of our names and shifts—except mine, which has been missing since she put me on probation. She disappears into her office for a moment before reappearing with the tiny magnet. With a flourish, she attaches it back to the board.

So I guess that's the end of that. Even though Naomi is on registers, I head back to the fruits, where I've been working this afternoon. I don't even glare at Greta. I smile and spray fruit with a water bottle. I unpack and line up kiwis and strawberries and

oranges so they look appealing. I direct customers who can't figure out how to weigh fruit on the nice scales provided to them. I'm
focused. I'm not going to think about money or Mom or Siobhan.
Not her freckles, the way her face scrunches up when she smiles,
the huskiness of her voice—

"Excuse me. Do you work here?"

I wince. It's an old white man. Old people are generally super
nice or super cranky. There's no in-between. This man has on a
pair of spotless white sneakers and has a tone of voice that tells
me he's looking for a fight. I paste the brightest smile I can muster
on my face.

"I do," I say, hoping I sound cheery enough. "How can I help
you?"

"I come here every week for my plums," he says, jabbing a
hand in the direction of the cantaloupe. "They're usually *right
there,* but now they aren't."

"Oh," I say, scratching the back of my head. "I'm sorry, but I
actually think we're out of plums. They might be out of season or
something."

"Or *something*?" His eye looks like it's twitching. "You can't
be serious."

"I am," I say. "We have so many other types of fruit, though.
I'm sure we'll be able to find something else you might like.
Maybe some pears? They're sort of like plums."

His face flushes and his toes tap against the floor. Oh dear
God.

"I don't think so," he says. "I'd like to see your manager."

Bill is already on the scene. He shoos me over to the registers,
probably so I can't make any more trouble. I glance at Greta's

door on my way over. Thankfully, she's talking on the phone, not paying attention to me. Technically, this doesn't count as a failure. I do better on registers anyway.

Naomi turns around to watch as I open my register.

"Wow," she says. "I think that's a record."

"A record for what?"

"For failing at fruit duty," she says. "What, that was five minutes?"

"I didn't *fail*," I say, folding my arms. "There was just a difficult customer."

I'm about to say something else, but my phone buzzes. I pull it out to see a new email and I can't help but grin. Instead of going to sleep at a decent time last night, I stayed up scrolling through Etsy, and found a tailor who said they could actually take my ideas for a dress and make it. My stomach does little somersaults at the news that they've actually started sketching the pattern.

Naomi stops talking to me to help a customer who comes over. To make it look like I'm working, I start bagging her groceries. We make an efficient team. As soon as the lady pushes her cart away, Naomi turns to me.

"Hey, do you wanna come over and watch a movie today?"

"I can't," I say. "I'm working a double shift."

Her eyebrows raise.

"What?"

"Nothing," she says, grabbing a magazine off the rack. "I didn't say anything."

"Listen," I say, batting my eyelashes at her. "I'm your best friend, right? So do you think I could start working some of your Friday shifts?"

Naomi blinks slowly, like an owl.

"With the party and this new dress and everything, I need the shifts," I say, tugging at my apron. "Except Fridays are already—"

"What do you mean, the new dress?" she says. "I thought we still had to look for one."

"I didn't tell you?" I tug a little at my collar. "I found someone on Etsy to make me one. I just have to send my measurements."

"Etsy?" Her lips wrinkle like she just sucked on a lemon. "I thought we were going to buy one together."

"I mean," I say. "It didn't exactly go well the first time. And they're charging three hundred bucks, which is only fifty dollars more."

Naomi glances down at her magazine for a moment that stretches on for too long.

"I didn't think it was a big deal," I say.

"I like working on Fridays," she says.

"Really?" I try my best not to fold my arms. "I didn't know that."

"Maybe you would," she says, looking back at the magazine, "if you ever asked about me anymore."

"What's that supposed to mean?"

"When's the last time we talked about me?" She glances up at me. "Or what I like? Or anything other than Siobhan and your party?"

"We talk about Cody—"

"We barely talked about Cody for five seconds when we were *at his house* before it became all about you and Siobhan."

"That's not fair," I say. "You could've said something—"

"I'm saying something now." Naomi slams the magazine back

on the rack. "I'm tired of talking about the party. I don't want to hear about it anymore. Okay?"

Something about her expression looks ugly. I take a deep breath.

"I'm going to have a really fun party," I say. "Why can't you just be happy for me?"

"I can't be happy about something that's not going to happen."

I jerk back, but her expression doesn't change. She doesn't even look apologetic.

At this point, it doesn't even feel like I need a party to announce who I am. But now that I'm officially dating Siobhan, I want to *celebrate* it. The party feels less about coming out and more about celebrating how happy I am to be queer—in a way I don't think it was before. But I don't know how to explain that to Naomi, especially right now, when she's so down on the whole thing.

How long has she thought this—since we came up with the idea? Since I started putting money away? Since she started making comments about money at Target and during our other shifts?

"You think I can't do it?"

"It's not about what you can and can't do," Naomi says. "It's just. A lot of money."

"For *me*."

"Well, yeah," she says. "It's a lot of money for you to come up with by yourself."

"You're right," I say. "I don't have rich parents to do everything for me."

"Is that what you think?" Her mouth twists. "That my parents do everything for me?"

"I don't know, Naomi," I say. "Not all of us have parents who will throw us a big party or buy us a car or pay for our college—"

"It's not my fault that I have money and you don't."

I feel about five seconds away from slapping her. It's only because of Bill that I don't. He walks up and stands between our registers, hands on his hips. Naomi quickly turns away.

"Is everything all right over here?"

My hands are shaking and my entire body feels hot. I kind of want to scream.

"Yeah," I croak. "Everything is fine."

CHAPTER 27

After the joy that is Saturday, I'm looking forward to a lazy Sunday, but my mother has other ideas—it's apparently a church Sunday. She wakes me up at eight on Sunday morning and tells me to put on a skirt. By the time I've rolled over to argue with her, she's already left the room, and I don't have any choice but to follow.

It was easier to like church back when I was little. Back in sixth grade, my Sunday school teacher was a big Black woman, super tall and round, who wore a beautiful headwrap every week. She always looked like royalty. Maybe I had a crush on her, too. Whatever.

I didn't stop believing for one particular reason, just a bunch of smaller ones: hearing about Tamir Rice and Eric Garner and Mike Brown and Sandra Bland, all the school shootings and the Parkland kids, my dad . . . It's like everything was shitty and I'd pray and nothing would get better. It didn't make any sense to me that God would let some humans be killed in school shootings or because of the color of their skin. What kind of God would do that?

So it's kind of hard for me to sit through church now. We sit in a pew and I have to listen to Mom talk to all her church friends, like Sister Rosa and Sister Martinique. I stand next to her and smile at them but tune out their conversation. They usually only talk to Mom anyway.

"How have you been doing, Mahalia?"

I blink over. Sister Rosa is staring right at me, like she can read my thoughts.

"I'm good."

"Everything going well in school?"

"Yeah," I say. "School is good."

I feel Mom glaring at me, but I don't know what else she wants me to say. It's not like I'm going to pour out all my sorrows to her church friends. Everyone knows that no one gossips like ladies at church.

The organ starts to play, so everyone settles into their seats. The stage is gigantic, with one of those big music systems and a band playing trumpets and saxophones in the corner. It's all very extra but Pastor Patrick always says you should spare no expense for God. There are girls around my age who sway and dance on-stage in dresses that look like nightgowns. I used to want to dance with them when I was little, but after I started having doubts about God, that dream went down the drain. Everyone starts singing and clapping. Mom leans down to whisper in my ear.

"I understand that you don't want to be here," she says. "But that doesn't mean you can be rude."

"I'm not being rude!"

She gives me a *look,* so I shut up.

Praise and Worship lasts for two hours and I'm not allowed to sit down for any of it. My legs are sore by the time Sister Mary appears onstage to do announcements, sharing news about who had a baby and who is getting married. I'm trying my absolute best not to fall asleep. Still, Mom keeps glancing at me every few seconds, like she's just waiting to slap the back of my head.

"Now," Sister Mary says, leaning up against the podium. I can barely see her face underneath her gigantic pink hat. "As you all know, Sister Leah has been having some trouble ever since she lost her job."

Oh God. I glance at Mom, but her expression is unreadable. This is why I never tell any of the ladies about my business. Why the hell would she let the whole congregation know about losing her job?

"These are hard times for all of us," Sister Mary continues. "So, if you could, please come up and put a few dollars in the collection box for Leah and her daughter."

I was expecting an awkward silence, for no one to move, but there's a decent line of people heading toward the stage. Of course, they take the chance to look over at us. Some people press hands to Mom's shoulders or murmur words of encouragement as they walk past.

"Keep your head up, baby," an older lady says to me. "Better days are coming."

It's nice and all . . . but they couldn't have done this in private? Now *everyone* knows Mom doesn't have a job. For the rest of the service, all I can do is sit on my anger. Most people know Mom had me as a teenager and that my dad isn't around. Now we're the charity case of the entire church. I don't need these people to feel bad for me.

After the four-hour service, I rush to the car while Mom goes up to the front and talks to Sister Mary and Pastor Patrick. It sounds stupid, but I actually feel like crying, and I don't know why. It's not like I'm sad. I'm just fucking embarrassed. As soon as I get in the car, I turn up Solange as loud as I can. I get through five songs before Mom comes out of the church. She's walking with a skip in her step, grinning.

"Why'd you take so long?" I ask as soon as she gets into the driver's seat. "I thought you were just going to get the money."

"And talk to the pastor," she says. There's an envelope in her hand and she waves it back and forth as she talks. "Two thousand dollars, Mahalia. That's how much they raised for us. Can you believe it? Thank God. We're so blessed to have so many people caring for us."

I blink. Two *thousand* dollars? Damn. Our church is pretty big, and it looked like a ton of people went up to give some money. It's actually . . . pretty nice. For the last few weeks, it's felt like we've barely been treading water, and this will be a big help. More of a help than my own father has been. But they shouldn't have to do this—we shouldn't be in a position where we need our entire congregation to help keep us afloat. Shame burns in my chest.

"And Sister Mary says she'll ask around, try to find some work for me," Mom continues, shoving the envelope in her purse. "It would probably be at a doctor's office, but that's better than nothing, isn't it? God is really looking out for us."

"I mean, isn't God the reason why you got fired in the first place?"

I wince as soon as the words are out of my mouth. Yeah, I'm crabby because she woke me up so early, because I had to sit through all of that for the first time in months. But I didn't have to go *that* far.

But Mom doesn't snap at me like I expected her to. Her smile barely twitches.

"God isn't the reason for all our struggles, baby," she says. "He always has a plan. Sometimes He just has something better in mind."

"Okay . . . ," I say, shifting so I can look at her face. "But why would He make you suffer just because? It doesn't make any sense to me. A God who loves you wouldn't want to hurt you."

"I'm not doing this with you right now." She shakes her head. "A good thing happened and we should be grateful our church cared enough about us to help us out. That's why church is so important. It's about God, but it's also about community."

"Community?" I scoff. "They gossip behind your back all the time. Did you even tell Sister Mary about losing your job?"

"Well—"

"Yeah," I say. I feel hot, like I've been sitting out in the sun too long. "I bet Sister Rosa said something to her as soon as she left our apartment when you were recovering. None of them can keep their mouths shut."

Mom pulls over so fast I almost break my neck.

"You have something in common, then," she says. "I'm sick and tired of this attitude, Mahalia. Why can't you just be grateful?"

"How come no one is grateful for what I did?" I snap, my hands shaking. "I've been working so many hours at the store to try to help out. I had to take care of you. And it's sh—really messed up that no one cares what I do but you care about what the gossip ladies at church do."

"Well, I'm sorry," she says. "I appreciate everything you've done for me. But maybe you shouldn't have done it if being acknowledged was so important."

"What?"

"Don't do things for people if you're just going to hold it over their head," she says, pulling away from the curb. "I didn't ask you to start working extra hours at the store. You could've kept saving for your party."

I'm about to tell her that she *did* ask me for money—for bills, for groceries, for things she couldn't pay for by herself. But for some reason, the thought makes my eyes sting.

"I couldn't just sit back and do nothing after you lost your job," I say, turning toward the window. "I'm not *that* bad of a daughter."

"Mahalia." She stares at me. "I never said you were a bad daughter."

I stare down at my lap.

"Why didn't you just tell me you were overwhelmed?" She places her hand on the back of my neck. "Did you think I wouldn't listen?"

"I don't know," I say. "You do a lot to take care of me, so I thought—"

"Well, that's because I'm the parent," she says. "And you're the child. Don't forget that."

I press my lips together.

"Listen, baby," she says. "It's hard. I understand. I wish I could make it better for you, but all I can do is my best. And that's all I want from you."

"I do try my best," I say. "It's just . . . frustrating. I don't know."

"I'm sorry I can't help with your party," she says. "I always thought I'd throw you one. My parents didn't believe in Sweet Sixteens, and by the time mine came around, I would've been too big for a dress anyway."

I glance up at her. She looks tired, but also open, like I could tell her anything. Sometimes I think about what it would be like to be pregnant now and I can't imagine it. I've been working my ass off for the past few weeks and it drove me crazy. But it's what my mom does all the time.

"It's okay," I say. "I'm still saving a little. I think I'll make it happen."

"Of course you will," she says. "I'm excited for you."

For some reason, her tone makes my heart drop to the pit of my stomach.

I don't know how to explain to her what makes the party so important. It's hard to even come up with the words myself. I think—at the beginning, I thought having a party would be a triumphant way to tell people that I'm queer, a way of proving that I don't care what anyone thinks about my identity. But I *do*. Even if I'm happy with Siobhan, even if I feel more secure in my queerness than I have in a while, I still care about what my mother thinks about me. I think I always will.

She puts the car into drive. I want to say something. I want to tell her that I wish we had more money, but not just because I don't want to worry about my phone bill or because I want a party. I wish she didn't have to work so hard, too. I wish she got to have a party when she was sixteen. But I think that might make both of us sad, so instead, I say nothing.

CHAPTER 28

After school and work on Monday, I feel extremely lucky to be sitting in Siobhan's room. Naomi and I haven't spoken since our fight, so I'm avoiding her. Things are awkward between Mom and me, too. We step around each other like roommates instead of mother and daughter. I'm not sure how to fix it—or even if I want to. Even though it's kind of shitty, I've been lying, telling her I'm at work when I'm here. I don't want to go into the whole *girlfriend* thing. The idea of having another heart-to-heart feels exhausting, especially since the last one didn't exactly go great.

Siobhan, on the other hand, is a haven. We're in her room, one of the nicest bedrooms I've ever seen. She has her window open, so you can smell the ocean, and the whole thing is painted a sort of teal green. There are little potted plants lined up on her desk and a Florence and the Machine poster over the bed.

There are photographs all over, pictures of Siobhan in Dublin with her friends, working in the garden, smiling at something just off-camera, her hair super fluffy and messed up. A picture of her with gigantic hair makes me smile. I want to ask her about all the pictures, to hear about Dublin and her grandparents and whatever a junior certificate is, but I also know I need to tell her about the dress before I chicken out.

"Wait," she says. "You need me to *measure* you? Is this a period movie?"

Just her saying the words out loud makes my cheeks flame.

"Are you asking because I'm European?" she continues, grinning way too much while I feel so awkward. "Because I promise this isn't a common occurrence for Ireland—at least, not in my neck of the woods. Maybe I was just missing out . . ."

"Come on," I say, even though I can't meet her eyes without feeling a laugh bubble up in my throat. "I just need my measurements for this dress and it's pretty hard to do it myself."

It shouldn't be a big deal—we're girlfriends now, after all. I don't even have to take my clothes off for her to use the measuring tape I stole from my mom's dresser.

"All right." Siobhan frowns down at the wikiHow article pulled up on my phone. "Start with the bust."

My mouth wobbles as she steps toward me, wrapping the thin piece of fabric around my chest, going under my arms and around my back. I don't know if I want to laugh or do something else. Instead, I focus on not looking at Siobhan.

"Of course," she says, sighing dramatically. "The first time I get to touch your boobs *would* be with your shirt on."

I snort. She grins at me, then lets the measuring tape fall, typing a number into my phone. It takes a beat for me to fully process what she's said—she wants to touch my boobs? I mean, of course she does. She said something like that at Cody's party. But now she's saying it *again,* sober, approaching me with the tape measure. Something warm grows in my belly.

"There now," she says. "I'm not so scary, am I?"

"I never thought you were scary," I say. I mean it as a joke, but it comes out softer than I expect.

Siobhan does my shoulders next—one end of the measuring tape on the tip of my left shoulder, drawing it across my back. She lets her hand stretch along with the tape, her fingers running across my shoulders. Even though I'm wearing a T-shirt and jeans, I shiver a little.

I don't think I've let myself think about how much I want her *this way* because I wasn't sure it was going to happen. But it's hard not to think about when she's touching me like this. Her hands are gentle, but firm, like she's trying to leave an imprint in my skin. When she pulls away to type, even for a second, my body sighs with the loss of her touch.

Her hands lower to my waist. She's standing behind me, so I can't see her, but I feel the way she gently squeezes my hips, almost possessive. Something hot and thick pools in my stomach like syrup.

"Siobhan," I say.

"Hang on," she says, her voice low. "Almost done."

But I don't want her to be done, is the thing. I want her to keep going. I don't want her to stop touching me.

"Can I look at you?"

"Not yet," she says. "I have to get your inseam."

I groan. She laughs, featherlight, and gently places both hands on my thighs. I think my brain whites out.

"Open up a little," she says, her voice still low. "It's from your crotch to your ankle."

Is she going to touch my crotch? Jesus. I did not think of this when I asked her to measure me.

"Actually, can you turn around?"

I turn awkwardly, slowly, like a foal taking its first steps. I know my face is on fire. I know I'm way too worked up over something as simple as my girlfriend measuring me for a dress. But then I see her face, how red and blotchy her cheeks are, how her hand shakes a little as she gently holds the tape against the inside of my thigh. Her hand is so close to my crotch. If she moved it just a little bit . . .

"Okay."

Siobhan sighs like she's been holding her breath this whole time, then turns toward her phone and types. Part of me is like, Wow, is that it? Am I the only one feeling . . . all of that? I'm trying to figure out a way to bring it up—to even form words when I feel so worked up—but then Siobhan drops her phone with a thud and our bodies press together, all thoughts flying out of my head.

Every inch of our bodies is touching, her hands gripping my hips, my arms locked around her neck. We've kissed before, but never like this. I feel like I'll die a little if we pull away.

"Mahalia," Siobhan breathes out. "Can I take off your shirt?"

"Why?" I say. "You want to see my epic boobs?"

"Yes." She grins, kisses me again. "Exactly."

I bite my lip for a second. As much as I've thought about it, I've never gotten this far with a girl before. For some reason, I can't stop thinking about what the woman at the dress shop said to me weeks ago—*try Lane Bryant*. Will Siobhan be turned off if she sees all the ripples of my body?

Siobhan kisses my cheek, then my neck, her finger tracing the bare skin just above my waistband.

"I can go first," she says into my neck. "If you want."

No way. If she goes first, I'll chicken out. With a deep breath, I force myself to peel off my shirt, tossing it to the floor in one swift movement. Siobhan's face splits into a grin. I cross my arms over my chest, but she shakes her head, stepping closer to pull them away.

"No, no, no," she murmurs. "That's not fair."

I'm not wearing anything sexy. My bra is missing a hook and I've had it for years. But Siobhan kisses me again, full of force, and I can feel how much she *wants* as she presses her body against me. It's overwhelming.

"Do you think," she says against my mouth, "I can convince you to take off the bra?"

"You know," I say, hands reaching behind my back, "you're very smooth, for someone who's never done this before."

"Smooth?" She snorts. "Are you my grandmother?"

"*Please* don't mention your grandmother right now."

My hands fumble around the clasp until she reaches behind me, her fingers covering mine. She catches my glance and gives me a shy smile. And when my bra comes off, I don't feel naked, not like I thought I would. Siobhan's gaze on me feels like a caress, leaving heat everywhere it touches. It's kind of insane—that she could want me as much as I want her.

"Mahalia," she says. "You're beautiful."

I kiss her again, everywhere this time: her eyelids and her cheeks and her neck and her chest, fumbling with her shirt so I can reach her boobs. Everywhere. And then she shows me how to do things to her with my fingers that I'd normally do to myself, in the shower or in my bed. She's soft and warm and as I watch her face, watch her eyebrows furrow and the way she works at her lip, I can't believe I'm doing this. I'm inside her, and it feels intimate in a way that's not allowed, like I haven't done enough to deserve it.

There aren't any gasping shrieks, and it makes me think I'm doing it wrong. But she grabs me and kisses me and makes this noise into my mouth and I know I'm doing it right. And when she blinks up at me after, a shiver rolls down my spine.

"Wow," she says. "That wasn't the period movie I was thinking about—definitely more *Bridgerton* than *Wuthering Heights*."

Then I shove her, even though we're both laughing.

* * *

"I actually have something I want to show you. But you can't make fun of me."

We're still in Siobhan's bed, legs tangled together, faced toward each other like we're the only people in the world.

"Mahalia," Siobhan says. "When have *I* ever made fun of you?"

I roll my eyes, but I can't stop grinning. I don't know how long we've been laying like this and I don't care. I could stay here forever.

"Come on," Siobhan says, pushing herself up. "Tell me what the big secret is."

"There isn't a big secret," I say. "I just sort of made a mixtape for you."

Her eyes crinkle around the edges. "A mixtape? Like in the eighties?"

"It's not actually a mixtape," I amend. "But it's like a playlist? On Spotify. I don't have my phone right now, so you could pull it up on yours . . ."

My voice trails off as she pulls out her phone.

"What's it called?"

"I mean," I say. "Here, let me find it."

Ultimately, even though I thought the playlist should have a super-special name of some sort, it ended up being called "Final Siobhan Playlist." Which isn't that romantic. But, honestly, that's what happens when the whole thing goes through three rounds of edits with your extremely judgmental best friend. The extremely judgmental best friend who I am currently not talking to.

"Oh my God," Siobhan says, peering over my shoulder. "Is St. Vincent on that? Let me see."

It's still kind of weird to be in her bed like this, no clothes, but she stretches past me for the phone like it isn't a big deal that our naked bodies press together. And it does feel kind of natural—or like it will be in the future.

"You're not allowed to laugh," I say as she takes the phone from me. "Like, you have to promise me right now, or I'll delete it in a fit of embarrassment."

"I promise not to laugh," she says, grinning at me. "When did you make it?"

"Um."

I don't know if I'm allowed to say I made it a little while after I met her or if that's too creepy. Thankfully, she hits play and "I

Prefer Your Love" by St. Vincent starts playing. Siobhan does a dramatic lip-sync, rubbing her hands all over her face and her hair like she's in a music video.

"Okay, no," I say, grabbing for the phone. "It's ruined. You just ruined it."

"Wait a minute," she says. "I want to see all the songs."

I try not to wince. I did my best to make the playlist a mix of songs we both know, but it's still a big deal to actually let her see it. The final playlist includes:

- "I Prefer Your Love" by St. Vincent

- "Edge of Seventeen" by Stevie Nicks

- "Make Me Feel" by Janelle Monáe

- "If It Isn't Love" by New Edition

- "The Only Exception" by Paramore

- "Don't You (Forget About Me)" by Simple Minds

- "Electric Relaxation" by A Tribe Called Quest

- "Just Can't Get Enough" by Depeche Mode

- "No Diggity" by Blackstreet

- "I Wanna Dance with Somebody" by Whitney Houston

- "Bad Reputation" by Joan Jett

- "Simply the Best" by Tina Turner

- "Lose My Breath" by Destiny's Child

- "Head Over Heels" by Tears for Fears

- "Every Little Thing She Does Is Magic" by the Police

- "Friday I'm in Love" by the Cure

"Sorry," I say. "I sort of made it before I knew you only liked music of the indie-rock persuasion. But I tried my best."

"Paramore *is* a little basic."

My eyebrows shoot up, but she's still grinning, delighted. It makes me smile, too.

"So you started making it a long time ago?"

"Why are you trying to get me to embarrass myself?"

"I'm not laughing," Siobhan says, even though she is, kind of. "I think it's extremely sweet. I'll listen to it until I'm tired of all the songs, and even then, I'll listen again."

She kisses my cheek with a grand flourish. My cheeks burn even though there's no one here but the two of us.

Siobhan must've hit shuffle, since the opening beats of "Electric Relaxation" fill the room after St. Vincent is finished. I glance at her out of the corner of my eye. She doesn't seem to recognize the song, which means she doesn't know it's about sex. But she will, if she listens to the lyrics. I'm suddenly regretting picking so many songs about sex.

Phife and Q-Tip are talking about being in a "horny state" and "pounding the poontang." I sink farther and farther into my spot on Siobhan's bed. She cocks her head to the side.

"What's a poontang?"

I cough. "Uh, it's like your vagina."

She starts to laugh. I want to laugh with her, but also, my cheeks are burning so hard my entire face could be on fire.

"Are you trying to tell me something, Mahalia?" she asks, leaning forward. She's close enough for our lips to touch. "Is there a hidden message?"

"I think," I say, "I already got that message across earlier when I—"

She kisses me then, and for a little while longer, I don't say anything at all.

CHAPTER 29

I don't notice the email at first when I get home. I'm too giddy, walking on air as I kick off my shoes at the front door, checking my mail app to see if the tailor on Etsy has gotten back to me about the dress measurements I sent. Being with Siobhan makes me feel like things are possible—like school will work itself out, like the future won't be a big mess, like I *will* get to have my party.

But then I see an email from the College Board.

I don't even open it—I make a beeline for my room, diving for my laptop. The few seconds it takes for the computer to connect to Wi-Fi feel like forever. I'm barely breathing, but I'm sure I'm about to be sick. My fingers are itching to text Naomi—but I don't. Instead, I log onto the College Board website and maneuver to my account almost on autopilot. When I finally find my score, it takes a few seconds for my brain to process the numbers.

700 out of 800 for English. I grin, but it doesn't last.

480 out of 800 for math.

Altogether, that's 1180—it seems a million miles away from the 1350 I was hoping for. I blink, expecting tears, but my eyes are dry. I'm just . . . numb.

I knew my score wouldn't be great. But I didn't think it would be lower than my PSAT. Is it because I didn't study enough? Because I didn't take the classes? Or just because this particular version of the test brought out all my weaknesses? I rub at my forehead, where deep frown lines have formed.

The web page has buttons directing me to sign up for a new test, but I still feel traumatized from the last one. The thought of taking it again—preparing forever, dreading it for weeks, and finally having to sit for a test I know will majorly impact my future—makes me want to go to sleep for several months. And it's obvious that studying by myself isn't working, so I'll actually have to find a class I can pay for, which means giving up more money—and time.

I grab one of my pillows in my hand and scream into it as loud as I can.

"Mahalia?"

My head snaps up. I didn't see Mom when I walked in a few minutes ago—has she been here the whole time? I rest my pillow in my lap and hope she was just admonishing me for screaming. But then she says my name again, her voice a little sharper, and I know something is up

God. Why is there always something up?

When Mom's on her game, she can sniff my bullshit out from miles away. I've never been able to get away with a major lie. It's like she can feel the lies formulating in my mind before the words even leave my mouth. She hasn't been paying me that much attention lately, but tonight, she's back to her old self. I can tell as soon as I step into the living room. She stands by the table, arms folded, an eyebrow raised. For a second, I'm sure she knows my SAT score. But that doesn't make any sense. Mom doesn't have access to my College Board account, and anyway, the SAT is something I've been navigating myself. No, this has to be something else.

"Mahalia," she says. "How was work?"

Shit. Does she know I was at Siobhan's? That feels like forever ago. Does Mom even *know* who Siobhan is?

"Uh," I say. "It was, uh, fine."

"That's funny," she says, cocking her head to the side, "since I didn't see you there when I had to pick up some tomatoes earlier."

I wince.

"We both know you weren't there," she continues, her voice casual. "But Naomi was very helpful. She said your shift ended early and you must've been spending time with your new friend."

My heart drops to my stomach.

I've never been able to picture coming out to Mom. Sometimes I think I'll do it once I move out and have my own career and don't need to depend on her. I have no idea how she'll react. Even though our current church is cool, in the past she's taken me to churches where pastors say homosexuality is a result of sin, and churches where they act like queer people just don't exist. During one of the few visits I ever had with my grandparents, my grandmother said I'd become a lesbian if Mom kept dressing me like a boy. Sure, Mom told Grandma off for being ridiculous, but I don't know if that means she's actually *okay* with me being gay.

"I just need you to explain this to me, because I really don't understand," she says. "You know how I feel about lying. I don't lie to you and you don't lie to me. Isn't that our agreement?"

"It is," I say. "But you lie by omission all the time."

Her eyebrows jerk up. It takes all my strength to keep myself from immediately apologizing.

"Excuse me?"

Mom barely spanked me when I was little, and I used to nod along with other Black kids when they mentioned whooping, like I knew what they meant. But something about the look Mom is giving me says I might not have to pretend anymore.

"You didn't tell me you were getting surgery until, like, the *day* it happened," I say, pulling the other dining chair out in front of me, even though I don't sit. "And you didn't tell me we were moving to a different apartment when I was ten until we did it. You didn't tell me Dad had a girlfriend until I first met her. There are a lot of things you don't tell me."

"That's because I'm the adult," she fires back. "And don't act like *you* tell *me* everything, Mahalia."

Normally I wouldn't participate in a stare-off with my mother. I'm pretty sure looking into her angry eyes for too long will set me on fire or something. But this time, *I'm* angry, too. I'm angry she's made promises she's had to break. I'm angry we don't live the life I wish we did. I'm angry at her even though I shouldn't be, since I know this isn't her fault. I'm angry because I know she's the safest to be angry at. But instead of yelling or making excuses, I surprise myself by saying exactly what's on my mind.

"Mom," I say. "I'm gay."

Her eye twitches. I wait another second, but she doesn't start screaming or calling me the spawn of the devil. On the other hand, it's not like she's smiling or pulling me in for a hug like I've seen white parents on TV do. I'm not sure what this means.

"Gay?"

"I mean." I take a seat across from her, folding my hands together. "I'm either gay or bi or maybe even pansexual but—I have a girlfriend. Her name is Siobhan."

She rubs her forehead so hard you would've thought I joined a gang.

"I don't know what pansexual means," she says.

"It's sort of like being bisexual," I say. "But—"

"If you're bisexual," she says, brow furrowed, "well . . . that means you could still be with a boy, doesn't it?"

I blink so hard it almost hurts.

"Well, no, because I'm dating Siobhan," I say. "And boys generally irritate me."

"But that's . . ." She shakes her head. "Sweetheart, boys are horrible at this age. When you get older, you might find a boy you like. Boys just need a little more time to mature. It's just that you're so young right now."

"That's not even the point," I say, willing myself not to snap. "I—I really like Siobhan and we're going out. That's what I'm trying to tell you about. That's what this is *about*."

"Does Naomi know about this?"

"About what? Siobhan?" I twist my mouth. "She does."

She nods. "Who else?"

"Um . . ." My voice trails off. "No one, really."

"Good."

"Good?" My eyebrows shoot up. "Mom, I told you I have a girlfriend, and you didn't even *ask* about her. Don't you want to know what she's like?"

Mom presses her lips tightly together.

"I think," she says slowly, "that you're too young for all of this."

"All of *what*?"

"Watch your tone with me," she says, a note of warning creeping into her voice. "I never decided if you were allowed to date or not."

She's not making any sense.

"I'm sixteen," I say. "I have a job. I drive. I help pay the bills. And I'm not old enough to date?"

Mom's eyes narrow.

"No, I'm not sure if you are," she says. "This is a big . . . you might be . . . confused. Why would you label yourself as gay when you aren't even . . . mature enough?"

Jesus.

"I'm not confused." I don't even try to keep my voice down. "You're not even making sense. Is there a magic age when I'm allowed to be gay? Do I have to be out of the house for you to be comfortable with my sexuality?"

Mom shakes her head, like I'm being ridiculous, and I want to scream in her face.

"You have to understand, Mahalia," she says. "It's not just me. It's—everyone would have something to say. Do you understand? Everyone at church would talk about it."

"Oh God," I say. "The church we go to once a month? I don't care what they have to say. I really don't. I want to know if *you're* going to give me a hard time if I bring my girlfriend home. I want to know that you won't look at me differently."

"How can I not?" Mom says. "You *are* different."

There's a lump in my throat. I shake my head. What did I expect?

"I'm going to my room," I say, picking up my bag. "I have homework."

She doesn't come after me.

CHAPTER 30

When I leave the apartment to go to school the next day, I finally feel like I can breathe. Sure, my mom isn't talking to me, my best friend isn't speaking to me, I practically failed the SAT, and I barely have enough money to buy a pair of shoes to go with my dress, let alone pay for my party. But I'll get to see Siobhan. That outweighs all the bad.

During history class, we lock eyes all throughout the period, smiling at each other while Mr. Willis makes us take practice AP exams. It's like Danny doesn't even exist—even though it's hard not to notice the way he looks at Siobhan like a kicked puppy. Sometimes she looks over at him, after she's flipped a page in the packet or while tapping her pencil against her chin, and something passes between them. I force myself to look down at my packet.

Which of the following movements from the period of 1870 to 1920 . . .

I glance back up. Danny is still looking at her, even though she's looked away. I dig my teeth into my lower lip and try to think of an essay I can write in the last five minutes of class. But it's next to impossible. Siobhan and I are happy together. She broke up with Danny so that she could be with me. There's no reason for this ugly feeling in my chest to exist—so why is it still there?

The bell rings, snapping me out of my thoughts. I gather my books as fast as I can. Even though Siobhan turns back to smile at me, it's too quick of a glance for her to notice my silent plea for her to stay. I try to ignore the way Danny glances over at me. Like . . . he smells something bad.

He couldn't know, right? We're not being obvious. Mostly because Siobhan isn't exactly out. I don't mind. It's not like I want to deal with the whole Danny thing anyway.

Before I can rush after her, Mr. Willis calls, "Mahalia?" I close my eyes and force back a sigh before he can hear it. Everyone else has already left the classroom, rushing to their next classes, or at least away from the stupid practice test. I turn toward him with my lips pressed tightly together.

"Take a seat," he says. "How are you?"

He scrunches up his face like it physically pains him to ask. I actually might groan. I already have Mr. Lewis trying to be a character from *The Blind Side*—I don't need another.

"I'm fine," I say, standing awkwardly in front of his desk. "But I have math—"

"I'll write you a pass," he says. "I just wanted to let you know—well, I've been grading the group projects."

I wince. At the beginning of every class, someone, usually Lindsay Rocha, asks why it's taken so long to get our grades back. Mr. Willis looks like he wants to quit his job every time she opens her mouth. Honestly, I don't blame him.

"I know group projects can be tough," he says, lowering his voice like he's sharing a secret. "But I'm impressed by your paper."

The paper that was basically a manifesto against the electoral college?

"Um," I say. "Are you sure?"

He shakes his head a little, a small smile on his face. It's weird enough for Mr. Willis to compliment me. But *smiling*? I wonder if he recently started antidepressants.

"I *am* sure," he says. "You remind me a lot of myself, you know."

I try my best not to make a face, but it's evidently not good enough. Mr. Willis actually *laughs.* I hold my books close to my chest like he just whipped out a knife.

"I know, I know," he says, pushing a coffee mug to the side. "Your boring history teacher isn't exactly someone you want to be compared to."

"Oh," I say, "I didn't mean—"

"No harm done." He holds up a hand, shaking his head. "I bring it up because I wrote about the electoral college for my college application."

"Really?" I blink hard. "They tell us we should write about a struggle we overcame or, like, why our lives suck or something."

"In a sense, I *did* do that," he says, smiling a little. "This is all a roundabout way of asking if you have any idea what your plans are for college. I studied history at Berkeley—I wouldn't mind looking over your essay and application, if you're interested in a similar path."

I try to picture Mr. Willis at Berkeley, smoking pot and talking about fighting the *man.*

"I actually want to study communications," I say, almost like an apology. "To work in radio."

Mr. Willis doesn't look disappointed like I expected. Instead, he cocks his head to the side, nodding thoughtfully.

"Interesting," he says. "Well, you have strong opinions—and strong communication skills. The offer still stands."

I shift my books in my hands.

I know it's not *weird* for a teacher to offer to help with college essays. But it's still . . . kind of weird when two offer in one week. Like I'm just so pitiful that teachers feel they *have* to help. It's hard to imagine actually taking him up on the offer, but Mr. Willis's offer seems more genuine somehow.

"What about . . ." I purse my lips. "Don't you have a ton of other work to do? Like grading and lesson plans and stuff?"

"Well, yes." Mr. Willis nods. "But I make time for students I believe in."

I try to ignore the little flare of pride in my chest at that, but it dies down when I think of my actual college prospects.

"That would be nice," I say slowly. "But you should know—I didn't score high on my SATs. My grades aren't high enough for me to be valedictorian or anything. And I think I need to start over on my essay."

"Well, that's what I'm here to help with," Mr. Willis says. "Mahalia, I think you're bright, and passionate, and I promise there aren't any prerequisites or expectations."

"Okay." My cheeks heat as I nod.

He pulls out a pad of passes.

"And," he adds, glancing at the clock as he fills in the form, "in my humble opinion, the SATs are bullshit. But don't tell anyone I said that."

I should laugh or smile at someone as uptight as Mr. Willis cursing in front of me, but I just hold my books a little tighter.

"And you're sure you still want to?" I hate how small my voice sounds. "Even when it comes to scholarships?"

His eyes dart up and lock on my gaze.

"I'm very sure, Mahalia," he says. "We can find some scholarship applications to work on, too, if that helps."

Part of me feels pitiful, standing at his desk, asking for help. But I've also had a shit time doing it alone. And if I have to pick between Mr. Willis and my English teacher, who collects kids of color like he's aiming to win a prize, I know who my choice will be.

"Okay," I say, taking the pass from him. "Thank you."

* * *

"There are people in the toilet," Siobhan says when I walk up to her. "All three of the stalls are filled."

Since getting together, we've started a routine. Every free period, we jet to the third-floor bathroom near the janitor's closet to make out. The only time girls come in here is to smoke or get ready for after-school sports.

"Shit," I say. I might feel a little too invigorated from my talk with Mr. Willis earlier. "We can check to see if anyone is in the band room."

"The band room?"

"It's the only classroom without a security camera," I say, lifting an eyebrow. "You can imagine how much people get *down* when they aren't having class—"

"Mahalia," Siobhan says. She's trying to look serious, but the corners of her mouth betray her. "I cannot believe you just said *get down*. I know your music tastes are stuck twenty years in the past—"

"*Okay,* no need to attack the Cure," I say. "How about a quickie on the football field?"

"Goodness, you need to be stopped." She shakes her head and tosses her arm around my shoulders. "How about you take me to this band room and we can negotiate the quickie there?"

"It was just a joke," I say, cheeks suddenly warm. "I didn't actually expect you to—"

"Sure," she says. "I *totally* believe you."

The late bell rings, signaling that everyone should be in their classes by now. The halls are practically empty. Siobhan looks both ways, grips my hand, and pulls me toward her. Before I can ask what she's doing, she kisses me. Right there in plain sight. It's really just a quick peck, but I still lean into it, still close my eyes. I like the feeling of being wrapped around her: her hair brushing against my cheek, the smell of her in my nose (maybe Irish tea?), the promise of her against my mouth. But when we pull apart, Siobhan doesn't meet my eyes. She's staring at something behind me. I turn my head.

It's Danny. His eyes are wide like he's just seen a ghost.

"Oh," I say.

"Danny," Siobhan says, snatching her arm from my shoulders. "Hey—"

"Are you *serious*?" He shakes his head. A little laugh, harsh and sharp, forces its way out of his mouth. "You've been gay this entire time? So why'd you go out with me in the first place?"

"Danny," Siobhan says again. "Come on, let's just talk. It's not that simple."

"I'm done talking," he says, backing away. "To *you*. Maybe someone else will wanna hear about your little girlfriend."

"What does that mean?" I butt in.

Danny doesn't answer. He's too busy walking away. Siobhan stares after him.

"Siobhan," I start.

"I . . ." She shakes her head. "I have to talk to him."

Talk to him about *what*? I don't get the chance to ask because she starts running after him.

"Shit," I say out loud. "Fuck."

I stand there, alone in the hallway, until the bell rings. I'm not going to my next class. I have no idea what I'm doing. I have no idea where I'm going.

Siobhan isn't out. I haven't had my party yet—I haven't been able to tell people about Siobhan the way I want to. And she seems worried—worried enough to run after Danny and leave me alone. I don't know what that means. Is she ashamed of me? Of being with another girl? She's been acting like it isn't a big deal ever since she broke up with him, but maybe that was just an act. Maybe it's different now that her ex-boyfriend is angry.

Fuck.

I don't want this to be reduced to school drama. I don't want our relationship to always be connected to Danny. I don't want people walking up to me and asking me questions or giving me weird looks. It'd be one thing if Siobhan and I just started holding hands in the hallway or going to school dances together, but if people think I somehow *stole* Danny Elliot's girlfriend, it'll be something else entirely. People will think I *turned her gay* or whatever. It sounds stupid, but I wouldn't put it past some of the kids at this school.

I can't talk to Naomi about this. I don't want to. She wouldn't really get it. And I obviously can't talk to my mom. So who else does that leave?

Before I know it, I'm walking out of school. The back door is already open for gym classes and no one notices as I pass the track in quick strides. I don't think they care. Once upon a time, it upset me that people barely gave me a second glance when I walked past, but now I'm used to it. I don't want people to whisper about me. I don't want to be the center of some weird story.

I keep walking and walking until, somehow, I end up at my father's house.

CHAPTER 31

I've only been to this house a few times before. My dad has an actual *house,* while we live in an apartment. It's not gigantic, nowhere near as nice as Naomi's, but it's still a house. Blue and small, with a brown roof and two cars parked in the driveway and big windows with flower beds outside. Jada must've planted them.

Inside, the windows are open, letting in sunlight and the occasional burst of wind. The walls are painted a light golden color. Things look pretty similar to Dad's old apartment—same couch, TV, speaker system. There are hallways leading to other rooms I haven't explored. I know Naomi's house better than this.

Jada is spread out on the floor with Reign and Legend in front of her. Legend rests on his belly, stares up at me with an open little mouth as I walk into the room. Reign stands with her hands on her hips and her hair in little braids clipped closed with beads. She practically glares at me.

"Mahalia," Jada says, lifting up her head. "I haven't seen you around in a while."

"Yeah," I say. My voice won't stop cracking. Fuck. I don't want to have family time with my younger half siblings or talk to

Jada. I just want . . . to cry to someone who isn't involved in any of the shit going on. And the first person I could think of was Dad.

Jada and Dad share a look. It's weird to see them acting like a couple, even though that's what they are. I probably should've thought twice before I came here. Seeing them makes me feel all sorts of things I don't know how to deal with.

"Reign," Jada says after a moment. "Say hi to your sister."

"Hi," Reign says. Then she dives into her mother's lap.

"I think Hallie and I are going out," Dad says, glancing at me for confirmation. I give the slightest bit of a nod. "For some bonding time."

"All right," Jada says. "Have fun, you two."

"Come on," Dad says, nudging me toward the door. "I know just the place."

* * *

Dad takes me to this old diner a few miles away. The old lady at the front smiles at him and he gestures for me to sit at the counter. When a young kid comes over to ask what we want, he orders a vanilla milkshake for himself and strawberry for me. I know he hasn't forgotten me, even though it feels like it sometimes, because he knows my favorite flavor and also that I hate to order.

This whole day is making me feel too many feelings. It's exhausting.

"I know I haven't seen you in a while," I say, rubbing my forehead. "Things have been rough lately and I . . ."

I trail off. I'm too old to expect him to make it all better. But that's why I came to him in the first place, isn't it?

"Yeah, we haven't talked in a minute," he says, not looking at me. "But your mom said you have some problems with me. I figured it would be best to give you space."

I hate that he phrases it that way. Yes, I do have problems with him, but he sounds defensive, not like he actually wants to talk about it. Dad has never really punished me or yelled, just passed all that stuff off to Mom. I have no idea how he treats his own kids. Maybe he spanks or maybe he doesn't. It's hard to think of him actually being around for their entire lives.

He slurps his milkshake. "We don't have to, if you don't want to. I've noticed that you've been a lot more distant these last few *years,* actually. Ever since you became a teenager, really."

"Well, you don't really see me," I say, stirring my straw. "So I guess you wouldn't know."

He pauses, placing the cup down. I'm not looking at his face.

"Your mother and I used to have a visitation schedule," he says, like he's choosing his words carefully. "But when you got older, you called and texted me whenever you wanted to see me, so I figured it wasn't necessary. When you stopped, I thought it would be best to give you your own time."

"But that's not how it works." I'm shaking my head before he even finishes. "You're my *dad.* You're supposed to be the one who reaches out, even if I'm not talking to you. When I'm mad at Mom because she grounded me or something, she doesn't just disappear."

"I didn't disappear," he says. "I've always been here."

"Yeah, well," I say, shifting in my seat. "It hasn't felt like that since . . ."

I can't say it. I'll just sound horrible if I say I think he's been ignoring me ever since he had more kids. I haven't said it to Mom. The only person I've said it to was Siobhan, and I don't want to think about her right now. She seems like the exception to every rule.

"Ever since what?"

I don't answer. Part of me regrets running to him when things got hard.

"Do you remember when I was in eighth grade?" I say, staring into my cup. Some ice cream has dripped onto the table. "And I had that big choir concert at the end of the year?"

"Um." His brow furrows. "I would've remembered that."

"Yeah, well," I say. "Jada went into labor with Reign that day. And, like, she wasn't born until the next day or whatever, but you still didn't come. Even though I told you about it for weeks. And when I called to ask where you were, you yelled at me."

I still remember, even though it was more than a few years ago. How I called him with tears in my throat and he acted like he didn't even have time for me. I got that he had a new family and everything, but how much would it have taken him to text and say he wasn't going to show up? People were walking around with their parents and grandparents who brought them flowers, who ran up to them after the show was over and told them how perfect they were. And I just had Mom, who had come straight from work and missed the first few songs. She missed my solo. No one was there to see me at all.

"Oh, Hallie."

Honestly, I don't even know if I want him to call me by that nickname anymore. I want to scream and yell at him. But there are already tears in my eyes and unloading all of this on him will make me cry harder than I have in a while. I can already tell.

"You weren't there," I say. "And it's, like, whatever now. I get you have other kids and everything."

It's not like I want him to move in or anything. But maybe it would mean something if I knew he was there, especially when no one else was.

"Mahalia," Dad says. "Look at me."

I push my straw to the side and take a gigantic gulp of my milkshake instead.

"Your brother and sister are not more important than you," he says. "I love you all the same. You're the one who made me a father. You've taught me more than they have."

"Okay," I say, putting my cup back down. "You know, it's not even that big of a deal—"

"I'm so sorry I missed your concert," he continues. "And I'm sorry for everything else I've missed. I figured I was doing the right thing by letting you decide when to see me, but maybe that was wrong."

He shakes his head, rubbing at his eyes.

"I don't know," he says. "My dad wasn't around. I'm not sure how to do this. I'm just trying to figure it out." I chew at my lip. I kind of get it. I have no idea what I'm doing, either. I just wish my parents did.

He's silent for a while, so long that our waitress passes by the table twice like she wants to ask if he's okay. I can't even tell if he's okay. I wanted him to be as upset as I am, but I didn't think he actually *would* be. Now that it seems like he is, I'm not sure how

I'm supposed to respond. When I think of *dads*, I think of people like Danny from *Full House* or Uncle Phil from *The Fresh Prince*. Not my dad, who looks like he could be my older brother, with his startled expression and Adidas sweatshirt.

I'm probably not ever gonna have a dad like Uncle Phil. But that doesn't mean I have to throw my whole dad away, right? Like, I could probably cut school and get milkshakes out of him more often. He's just not on the same level as Mom. I've always sort of known that, too.

"I'm going to be better now," Dad says, finally breaking the silence. He clears his throat. "I'll never miss a choir concert again."

"I mean," I say. "I'm not in choir anymore. But it would be nice if . . . if you could be around more. Even if I don't text you and ask."

"Right." He takes a deep breath. "You could come over for dinner, maybe. I don't remember the last time you came over."

"I don't know," I say. "Won't you be too busy with Reign and Legend?"

"No," he says. "And anyway, you and I can do things I can't do with Reign and Legend. We can watch R-rated movies. You could drive me around."

I snort.

"Sometimes I can't believe how fast you grew up," he says. "I thought I'd have more time."

Oh God. He's blinking really fast.

"Dad," I say. "I'm sixteen. Not thirty."

"Soon you will be." He shakes his head like he's made up his mind. "And I'm not going to miss any more of it. I promise."

I'm not sure how much I believe him, but it's nice to hear it, at least right now. I clear my throat and push my milkshake cup away.

"Could you give me a ride back to school?" I ask. "I kind of walked out when I wasn't supposed to."

His mouth twists as he looks out the window.

"God, I don't know, Hallie," he says. "I think Jada really needs me back. I don't leave her alone with the babies too often. It can be overwhelming for her."

"It'll only be like ten minutes."

Dad runs a hand over his head.

"Reign's been having a *really* hard time with tantrums lately. Maybe you could take the bus this time, and . . ."

He starts digging around in his pockets. I hate myself for the tears that pool in my eyes. There it is. He makes these promises and then pulls back at the smallest request. I'm barely asking for anything and he *still* can't follow through.

"It's fine." I shake my head and stand up. "I can just walk."

"Hallie—"

"Can you *not* call me that anymore?" I snap. "My name is Mahalia."

I don't expect him to follow me out of the diner, but it still hurts when he doesn't.

CHAPTER 32

I'm not sure how long it takes me to get back home and I don't care. There's no one around when I let myself in the apartment, just like there never is. I'm sweaty and maybe I'm still crying a bit when I throw open the door to my room and toss myself on the bed. Before I can properly indulge myself in a crying fest, my phone buzzes. For a second, my chest fills with hope, sure that it's Siobhan.

But no. It's just a reminder to pay the party venue by this Friday. I laugh bitterly, tossing my phone toward the end of my bed. I didn't even manage to save enough for the venue, let alone everything else. Why did I think I'd be able to save all that money by myself? I've been so stupid—not just about the party, but about everything. Dad wasn't going to completely change after talking to me in a diner for an hour. Naomi is going to stay mad at me forever and I'll never get to spend another afternoon at her house after school again. I made a mistake telling Mom that I'm queer—now things are going to be awkward between us forever. And I probably won't get any scholarships for college because of my SAT score, so I'll be stuck here.

None of the people who care about me are talking to me. By now, I'm sure Danny has told everyone about Siobhan and me.

Even if I *were* able to come up with the money for a party, I doubt anyone would come. I've been kidding myself this entire time. Instead of tossing my head into my pillow, I force myself up and pull the shoe box out from underneath my bed. It's stuffed with all my party crap—invitations, decorations, sketches of the dress I ordered. I pull the sketches out a little too roughly and they tear at the bottom.

I suck in a shaky breath. Of course. The dress is already being made, but it's not like I'll have anywhere to wear it. There's no way a party is still happening. I crumple the sketches in my hand and rip them clean in half. Then I rip them again and again and again until the pieces are too small to tear. The invitations are next—I take them out of their packaging and pull them apart. Before I know it, I'm out of breath, surrounded by tiny shreds of my doomed party.

"Mahalia?"

Mom knocks at my door, even though it's open. I rush to shove the pieces back into the shoe box. I'm so used to her being gone all day that I forgot she was only at a job interview.

"Hold on," I say. "Just one second."

She steps into my room anyway. I can feel her staring at the box in my hands.

"What's all this?"

I rub at my face and refuse to look at her. God, I'm so embarrassing.

"Nothing," I say. I even *sound* like I've been falling apart. "Just homework."

Mom is quiet. If it were anyone else, I'd think they'd left, but I can still feel her presence behind me.

"Your father called," she finally says. "He said the two of you had a little visit while you were supposed to be at school."

God, I can't handle getting in trouble now.

"I didn't feel well," I say, shoving the cover back on the box. "And I knew you were at the job interview and I didn't want to ruin it. But everything is fine now."

She's silent for another long moment. I wish she would just go away.

"I'm sorry you're having a hard time, baby," she says. "Will you look at me?"

My lower lip starts trembling. I feel her sit down on the bed.

"I'm sorry about your party," she says. "I'm sorry about everything. It's been tough for you."

Fuck, I'm crying again. Mom tugs at my arm and pulls me up onto the bed. She wraps her arms around me and rocks the two of us back and forth.

"You've had to grow up so quickly," she says, her mouth close to my ear. "I feel like you never had the chance to be a child and I wish I could slow it down. We'll never get that time back."

The last time I cried in front of my mother was in the eighth grade, when my dad didn't show up at that choir concert. There was this really intense look in her eyes and I could tell it bothered her. After that, I decided I was too old to cry in front of my mother. But I'm breaking that rule today. I open my mouth to say something, but I just make this little animal sound instead.

"Oh, honey," she says, squeezing me tight. "I'm sorry. I'm sorry about . . . I know I didn't react the way you wanted me to last night."

"No." I wipe at my nose. "You were really weird."

"I just . . . I was surprised." I feel a strand of her hair tickle my forehead. "I had so many questions. What if you want children? What does it even mean, to be attracted to boys and girls *both*? How does that work once you get into a relationship?"

When other kids come out, their parents smile and say they just *knew.* But I guess my mom didn't. She seems to know how everything works *except* me.

"Being bi doesn't mean you want to date two people at once," I mumble, my throat sore. "It's just—"

"I know," Mom says, her voice soft. "I looked it up. I want— I'm trying to understand."

Oh. I pull back to look at her. She smiles a little, embarrassed.

"So," she says. "You still like boys, but now you like girls."

I nod. Then the rest of it comes out before I can stop it—how I lied about the Sweet Sixteen, how the party is really for me to come out to everyone, why Naomi and I aren't talking anymore.

"I even ordered this stupid rainbow dress," I say, laughing wetly. "But I guess I don't have anywhere to wear it."

Mom is quiet for a long time. For a moment, I'm sure I've pissed her off. I'm sure she's mad I lied to her about something this big and was going to use her money for a party based on that lie. But when I look up, she looks a little like she wants to laugh and is trying her best not to.

"A party to announce that you are gay—*bi.*" She chews her lip, scratching a little at the back of her head. "That's . . . certainly . . . very special."

I burst into laughter. She looks shocked for a moment.

"What?" she says. "I'm *trying,* Mahalia."

I launch myself back into her chest. Her arms automatically wrap around me.

"I know, Mom. A for effort," I say. I can't remember the last time she held me like this, but it feels nice.

"I'm sorry," she says. "That you couldn't have your bisexual party."

I laugh and feel her chest shaking underneath mine.

"It's okay," I say, even though I'm not sure it is. "Maybe you can throw one for your next kid—maybe that one will be gay, too."

"Girl, please." She laughs so loud it almost startles me off the bed. "I don't have a uterus anymore. The baby factory is closed."

For the first time, I wonder how Mom must feel. Dad met someone else and had two more kids and Mom never will. Is that sad? I can't tell. Mom, on the other hand, has clearly made her mind up. She laughs again and says, "Thank *God.*"

I relax. Things feel easier, something in the air has lifted.

"I'm not a bad kid," I point out. "It could be so much worse."

"It could be," she says, eyes softening. "I'm lucky I was blessed with you. You're my only, baby."

"Yeah," I say, leaning my head on her shoulder. "You're my only, too."

"Now," Mom says. "Tell me about her?"

"About who?"

Mom scoffs.

"This girlfriend of yours, of course."

I feel warmed from the inside out.

CHAPTER 33

I'm pretty sure you can't trust any white person who has an un-
healthy obsession with *To Kill a Mockingbird*. It's not a proven sci-
entific theory or anything, but on Wednesday, when Mr. Lewis
starts class by announcing that his kids are Atticus and Harper, it
makes me side-eye him.

Naomi sits only a few seats away from me in this class. We'd
normally make fun of Mr. Lewis together—secretly texting under
his nose or making faces at each other—but she isn't looking at
me right now. I think about texting Siobhan, but we've barely spoken since yesterday.

I'm scared, she texted me after school. And what was I supposed to say to that? It's like the threat of Danny saying something has blown all the air out of our relationship. I don't know
what to do to fix it.

"This is a worthwhile book, isn't it?" Mr. Lewis says, leaning
against his desk. "It was one of my favorites at your age. I feel like
it taught me so much about the world."

I stare down at my desk and try not to draw any attention
to myself.

Mr. Lewis calls on another student. "Yes, Ashley?"

"I didn't expect to like it," Ashley says. "But I really relate to Scout. She reminded me a lot of myself when I was younger."

"Good, good," Mr. Lewis says, clasping his hands together. "Anyone else? Jake?"

"I liked Atticus," Jake says. "He was pretty badass."

"And I feel like you learned a lot about racism." I turn to see the owner of the voice: Rebecca Sinclair, *another* white kid. The only people talking during this conversation are white kids— Naomi and I are the only Black people here, and Naomi confirms my feelings by sighing loudly.

"Naomi?" Mr. Lewis says, holding his hands out toward her. "Do you have something you want to add?"

"Oh," she says, shifting back in her seat. "No, that's okay."

Yikes. Once Mr. Lewis locks onto someone, there's no chance of them getting away. I glance up at the clock above the board. Fifteen more minutes. We can do this.

"Come on," he says. "You read the entire book and didn't think *anything* at all?"

I know he's just teasing, but it makes me angry for some reason. I think about him making me stay after school. I don't know what's going on inside Mr. Lewis's head, but whatever it is, I don't like it. I'm about to open up my mouth and say something, but Naomi surprises me.

"It wasn't my favorite read," she says. "The story is all about Black people, but you don't really *hear* from them. We see the story through the eyes of someone whose opinion we don't really need."

Mr. Lewis blinks several times at that, like Naomi just said something crazy. I, on the other hand, want to get up and give her a high five. Instead, I turn and smile at her. She makes eye contact, just for a quick second, but there's a little smile on her face, too.

"Well, that's a valid perspective," he says, sitting on his desk now. "But the point is that we're seeing how racism needs to be combated in Scout's community. Her father is opening her eyes up to this issue and showing her how she can do her part to stop it."

"Yeah," Rebecca says. "I think Scout has to be the one telling the story because she's the only one who doesn't really understand."

Another kid joins in, and the conversation has moved on. Naomi sinks down in her seat.

No way.

Sure, Naomi and I haven't been talking, but I know that was a big deal for her to do. And I actually hate that we've moved past her point like she didn't say anything. I'm honestly irritated that we had to read this book at all, if the discussion was always going to be so limited. We literally could be reading the Toni Morrison ghost book right now.

"Actually, I agree with Naomi," I say without raising my hand. "It can be really annoying to read a book about a white girl learning about racism when you've experienced it your whole life. And the Black characters aren't even fully fleshed out, not the same way the white ones are. It made me angry."

"Well," Mr. Lewis says. That's all he says for a moment: *Well.*

No one else in class says anything. I kind of wonder if anyone else actually read the book, or if it was just the same three kids who *always* do all the homework. I wonder if they thought that deeply about the way the Black characters were presented.

"It was also disappointing to read about another Black man being killed," Naomi adds. "I thought maybe he would survive, but he didn't, and I don't know what the point was. That the town is racist? But, like Mahalia said, we already knew that. I don't think I learned anything new about racism from reading this."

"Well, I'm glad to hear from so many new voices participating in class today," Mr. Lewis says. "But I do want to encourage you to consider the time this was written in. It was 1960. When this book was released, what Lee was writing was radical. Almost no one could imagine a white woman saying these things about the South."

"I guess," I say, shrugging. "But things are different now."

Naomi catches my eye and winks at me. I grin back.

* * *

"I didn't expect Mr. Lewis to have a discussion about race with us, but God, I thought it would've gone a little better than it did."

Naomi and I are walking out to the student parking lot, arm in arm. I can't stop grinning.

"I just feel like don't teach a book about race if you don't want to talk about it," I say. "Like, all he ever talked about was how *good* Atticus is. I don't care about one white guy being good. I want to read about the Black characters."

"We should've read *Beloved* like Ms. Tatum's class."

"Right?" I gasp. "I was totally thinking that."

"It would've been so much better," Naomi says, shaking her head. "Or he could've at least picked a *single* book by a Black author."

We stop walking because we've reached her car. I don't want to let go of her arm.

"He's so obsessed with that book," I say. "I don't get it at all."

"White people are always obsessed with books like that," Naomi says, giving me a look that says *duh*. "Seriously, remember when *The Help* came out and everyone was obsessed with it? If he could get away with it, I'm sure Mr. Lewis would put it on the reading list."

"You're right." I bite my lip. "Viola Davis in *The Help* is basically Calpurnia."

"I know we just read the book, but I honestly can't remember anything about Calpurnia," Naomi says. "She doesn't get enough scenes."

She goes quiet, glancing at her car, then back at me. I shove my hands in my pockets.

"I'm sorry," I say. "For being a jerk to you and not listening when you told me about Cody and for being a shitty friend."

"No, I'm sorry." Naomi shakes her head. "I shouldn't have said all those things about your party and money. You're right. I don't have to worry about it the way you do. But I'm sure your party will be amazing."

"No, I don't think so." I bite my lip. "The deadline is this Friday and there's no way I'll have enough by then."

"Fuck." Naomi's face falls. "I'm so sorry."

"It's fine." I blink really fast so I don't start to tear up again. "Seriously."

She glances back at her car.

"Do you wanna come over after work?" she asks, almost shy.

"We can watch *The Half of It*. I'll tell you more about Cody. You can tell me about Siobhan."

My heart hurts a little. Siobhan and I aren't broken up—at least, I don't think we are—but things are nothing like they were the first few days we started dating. But it'll be nice to finally talk to my best friend about it.

"Naomi." I can't help but smile. "Do you even have to ask?"

CHAPTER 34

Every once in a while, the school administration forces us into the auditorium for an assembly. Sometimes it's just the principal reinforcing a bunch of boring rules or encouraging us to *try our very best*. Sometimes they bring in a guest speaker to talk about career paths. Today is truly the worst, though: they've hired a speaker to talk about why we should say no to drugs and alcohol.

"These things derail your lives. At your ages, you should be thinking about your future," a balding man dressed in khakis says, using a laser pointer to aggressively circle the slideshow projected behind him. "If you think of your life as one big road, alcohol and marijuana are like roadblocks or detours that push you off course—but so much worse . . . like a tornado or a hurricane."

I snort a little into my fist. Smoking pot is the equivalent of a hurricane wreaking havoc on my life? I'm not so sure about that. Naomi sits a few rows ahead of me with her own homeroom class. When she turns back to look at me, we both roll our eyes and pretend to gag.

"And now," the man says, "several of your classmates will join me onstage to act out a scenario that some of you might find your-selves in."

Three students awkwardly make their way onto the stage: Lindsay Rocha (of *course*), a girl from the drama club whose name I can't remember, and Danny. Which is . . . definitely a *choice*. I assumed Lindsay and the drama club representative must've vol-unteered for this opportunity, but seeing Danny up there makes me wonder if they were somehow blackmailed into volunteering.

"I am a down-on-her-luck student," Lindsay says into a micro-phone.

"I am a student drug dealer," Danny says, sounding dead inside.

"And *I* am a *bystander*," the drama club geek says, overenunci-ating each word.

I heave a heavy sigh and slide down into my seat.

My homeroom teacher, Mrs. Tell, isn't very interested in the whole thing. She's sitting in her seat reading a book with a big Reese's Book Club logo on it. I turn back to my phone. It's open to my conversation with Siobhan—the last thing I said was *Let me try to make it better.* Siobhan responded, *How? It's not even your call. It's Danny's.*

There's not much I can do to argue with that. Still, I ache to talk to her. Naomi told me I just need to give her time. I want to believe that'll help, but until we can figure out what Danny plans to do, we're stuck in this weird limbo.

"Greetings, fellow student, would you like to purchase some LSD?" Danny says in a monotone voice. "Ecstasy? Molly?"

"More enthusiasm!" the balding man yells.

I drop my face in my hands and groan. I truly can't handle this—I don't even want to *look* at Danny. Instead of allowing my brain to be melted by the rest of this insultingly terrible play, I dig into my backpack, pulling out a notebook. It's extremely corny, I know, but I rip out a piece of paper and write Siobhan's name at the top. In big letters, I write, *I'M STILL IN IF YOU ARE.* Then I fold it up.

When I pass the note to the kid next to me and point to Siobhan, he rolls his eyes and doesn't make an effort to move.

"Come on," I hiss. "Seriously?"

"Oh no," the drama student yells into the mic. "My *friend* has been *bamboozled* into taking LSD and Molly! Whatever shall I do!"

The kid next to me winces. Then, I guess because he feels bad, he passes the note along. I watch as people hand the paper on, occasionally looking back at me. Sometimes I smile and wave. When it finally reaches Siobhan, the person sitting next to her leans forward and whispers something to her.

Siobhan looks over at me. I wave. She rolls her eyes, opening the note. I don't exactly feel *nervous* about how she'll react. But when she looks up and gives me an exaggerated thumbs-up, I can't help but beam back at her.

God. We are the corniest.

The shrieking of a microphone makes my head snap back to the stage. Danny's marching angrily to the front. Is this part of the play? Is he going to force the bystander to take Molly, too? Jesus.

"Young man," the presenter says. "This isn't in the script. You're supposed to threaten your customer and—"

"Are you *serious*?" Danny snaps. But he's not speaking to the presenter or any of the cast members. He's looking right at me, nostrils flaring as he glances back at Siobhan. "You're passing fucking love letters?"

My stomach drops.

Fuck.

"Um," Lindsay Rocha says. "Am I in love with my drug dealer now?"

"Listen up, everyone," Danny says. "I have something to tell you all. Something pretty fucking scandalous, if you ask me."

I shoot up out of my seat just as the rest of the auditorium breaks out into mild chaos. Everyone is talking at once—a group of jocks are cheering, egging him on. Some people are giggling. Others *booooo.* The presenter's mouth is moving, but the sound of the crowd is drowning him out. Someone must've turned off his mic. When I glance at the back of the room, a group of AV Club nerds are clustered near the doors, waving up at Danny like they're his groupies.

What the *fuck* is he doing? Every inch of my body is sweating. I can't tell if I'm going to puke or bolt. What can I do? Jump up on the stage to tackle him? Just as I push my way to the edge of our row, Mrs. Tell blocks my way.

"Ladies and gentlemen, take a seat," Mrs. Tell says, holding her open book to her chest. "I'm sure this will be handled momentarily."

If anything, the wild sounds of the auditorium grow *louder.* Naomi's head whips back as she turns to me. I can't hear her, but I can tell what she's asking—"What are you going to do?"

I have no fucking idea. It all seems to happen in slow motion:

Danny, bringing the microphone back to his lips. A group of teachers marching toward the stage. They're not going to make it in time. He's going to ruin *everything*.

"Mahalia." Mrs. Tell is ordering now. "Please take a seat."

I can't. I can't take a seat. I have to stop him. But I can't—it's too late. Danny is going to do it. He's going to—

"HOLD ON!"

The chatter doesn't completely die down, but it does get a little quiet. I turn toward the voice. It's Siobhan, across the auditorium to my far left. She's standing on one of the red theater seats, precariously balancing on the armrests, wearing Birkenstocks with socks and a pair of green overalls. Her face is as red as I've ever seen it.

I hold my breath. Siobhan opens her mouth and begins to sing, loudly:

"I don't care if Monday's blue / Tuesday's grey and Wednesday too—" Her voice rises to a shriek. *"Thursday, I don't care about you / It's Friday, I'm in love!"*

Other students' heads whip back and forth as they whisper. Danny stares at her like she's grown a second head. Even the teachers are frozen. If I thought the auditorium was quiet before, it's deathly silent now.

"Monday you can fall apart / Tuesday, Wednesday break my heart," she continues. She's rocking back and forth like she might pass out. She's not hitting any of the notes. She looks fucking *ridiculous*.

Oh God. I love her so much.

"Saturday, wait / And Sunday always comes too late," I sing-yell as loud as I can. *"But Friday, never hes-i-tate."*

She turns toward me, grinning with her entire face.

"Dressed up to the eyes / It's a wonderful surprise / To see your shoes and your spirits rise," we sing together, our voices pushing and pressing against each other. They don't exactly fit, but it doesn't matter. *"Throw out your frown / And just smile at the sound / Sleek as a shriek, spinning 'round and 'round."*

Naomi jumps to her feet, clapping to the beat with her hands in the air. Cody jerks to his feet next to her. The kid next to *him* stands up. Before I know it, other kids are standing, clapping along to a song they probably don't know. Even Mrs. Tell smiles a little.

"Hey," Danny says from the stage, drowning out some of the lyrics. "Hey, don't you guys care that—"

"It's such a gorgeous sight / To see you eat in the middle of the night," Siobhan sings even louder, if that's possible, tossing her head up and down as she shreds on an air guitar. *"You can never get enough / Enough of this stuff."*

Out of the corner of my eye, I can see Mr. Willis escorting Danny and his castmates off the stage, but it doesn't matter anymore. Siobhan and I scream *"It's Friday, I'm in LOVE!"* in the loudest voices we can muster. She points at me, grinning like she has a secret, and the auditorium erupts into cheers and laughter. I throw my hands up in the air and toss my head back.

The buoyant feeling I get whenever I listen to my favorite song or yell the lyrics out my car window is back, but magnified a thousand times, filling up a gigantic space inside my chest. Filling the entire auditorium.

"All right, all right." Principal Oates is onstage now. "Back to your seats, everyone, or we'll have to seriously consider canceling junior prom."

I roll my eyes, but I can't stop grinning. Siobhan holds her hand out, dramatically reaching for me, and I laugh and do the same. The teachers and adults are all talking, but I can't hear them.

It's Friday and I'm in love.

CHAPTER 35

I'm not used to having weekends off. I'm pretty sure this is the first Saturday I haven't had to work in a month—and I definitely feel it. I'm halfway into my Fresh Abundance apron before I realize the only place I have to go is Naomi's house to hang out.

I wander into the kitchen to grab cereal. Mom is already up, leaning against the counter, staring at her phone like it's something from outer space.

"Mom?" I'm almost afraid to go near her. "Is everything okay?"

There could be a million things wrong—maybe we're getting evicted or the job interview went badly or she's dealing with some shit from my dad. But when she looks up at me, she's grinning, the biggest smile I've ever seen on her face.

"Mahalia," she says. "I got a job."

I jump up in the air and shriek. She laughs, tossing her head back.

"Jada called me the other day," she says. "After you went to your father's house."

"Oh." I scratch the back of my head. "She did?"

"The hospital she works at has an opening," she says, grinning. "She put in a good word for me, and when I went to the interview yesterday, they told me the job was mine."

If I'm being honest, I don't know much about Jada—I haven't taken the time to get to know her. I know she has a job at a hospital, but I'm not really sure what she does, and I've never really asked. But Mom has been going to interviews all week—this is the first one that's worked out. And we have Jada to thank for that.

"That's amazing," I say. My brain feels like it's moving in slow motion. "I—wow."

"Wow," Mom repeats. I squeeze her again.

"When I get back from Naomi's," I say, pulling away, "we totally have to celebrate."

Her eyes look me up and down. I'm not wearing anything *horrible*—just shorts and flip-flops. But Mom frowns. It's so quick, I'm not sure whether I imagined it or not.

"Something came for you," she says, disappearing into the hallway closet. "I put it away so that I wouldn't forget . . ."

Her voice trails off before she returns with a box. Etsy doesn't brand their boxes with a logo, but I can already tell what it's going to be, and my stomach drops. I step away from the box like it's going to burn me.

"Oh," I say. "Thanks."

But I don't move to touch it. Mom looks like she's going to ask something, so I just step toward the door. I don't want to explain what it is—bringing up the party will only make her feel guilty and there's no reason for that. I've barely opened the door when Mom says, "Wait."

I turn back and she practically yanks the keys out of my hand. "Let me drive you."

"Um . . ."

"Come on," she says. "It'll give us some time to bond before I have to go back to work."

I'm not sure how her driving me to Naomi's house counts as *bonding,* but I'm not about to say that. Mom shoos me out the door. I head toward the car while she locks up.

"Oh God." I gasp as I buckle my seat belt. "Are you seeing someone?"

"Come on, Mahalia." She scoffs, turning the wheel. "Be serious."

But this actually could be serious. Maybe she met someone on Christian Mingle or something and I just don't know about it. I could see Mom keeping something like that from me.

"I am," I say, glaring at her. "Are you?"

"I am not seeing anyone, Mahalia." She waves a hand. "I promise, if I were, you'd be the first one to know."

I still stare at her for a little bit longer, but she doesn't take her eyes off the road. By the time Mom pulls up to Naomi's house, there are already a bunch of cars parked in the driveway and out in front of the street. I blink rapidly. Neither of Naomi's siblings has a birthday today. Her brother isn't graduating from college yet. Maybe it's her mom's or dad's birthday—but wouldn't she have told me that?

"Mom," I say, glaring at her. "Are you getting married?"

"Mahalia, we've established that I'm not with anyone." She shakes her head. "I can't believe that's where your mind goes first. Now come on, get out of the car."

I do, cautiously. When I turn around, though, she's walking behind me.

"Mom," I say. "No offense, but Naomi and I are hanging out together. Just the two of us."

"I know that."

Instead of getting back inside the car, though, she walks briskly toward the front door. Like she's supposed to be here. Oh God. Is she going to have some sort of intervention for me? I don't think Naomi's parents would go for that super-Christian stuff, though. But maybe Mom fooled them.

"Mom," I say. "Come on."

The door is open—another odd thing. Mom steps inside like she lives here. With a sigh, I follow behind her. This is going to be so embarrassing.

As soon as I step inside, I'm blinded by rainbow-colored streamers.

"Surprise!"

I almost fall on my ass. There's a crowd of people in front of me, some faces I recognize, and some I don't—there's Naomi and her family, the crying guy from the store, Jada and the kids, Siobhan and her parents. More than a handful of other kids from school. It looks like the room is stuffed full.

From the doorway, I can't see much, but there's a gigantic banner taking up one side of the wall. In big pink, purple, and blue letters, it reads, *HAPPY COMING-OUT, MAHALIA!* And if I'm not mistaken, those are the familiar opening notes of "I'm Coming Out" playing from a speaker somewhere.

I immediately burst into tears.

For a moment, everyone is silent. I can feel a million pairs of eyes looking at me. Then Mom sweeps me into her arms, holding me so tight I might actually explode. Somewhere behind me, I hear Mrs. Sanders hushing people, forcing them to move to the empty side of the room.

"Baby," Mom says, only loud enough for me to hear. "I thought this was what you wanted?"

I'm crying so hard I can't even make out words. But the truth is, this *is* what I wanted—not exactly what I planned, but still somehow perfect all the same. I'd just given up on the idea that I'd ever get it.

Mom lets me blubber for a few more seconds before pulling back, swiftly wiping the tear tracks off my cheeks. She's holding my shoulders tight enough to leave marks.

"Mahalia Eve Harris," she says. "You are going to put on that big beautiful dress. You are going to dance the night away. And you. Are. Going. To. Enjoy. This. Party. Am I clear?"

I sniffle once more and Mom shakes me. Out of nowhere, I snort. None of this—her ordering me to have fun at my own party while my guests cower to Diana Ross in the background—makes any sense. Mom's face breaks out into a grin. Then we're both laughing, so hard it leaves an ache in my gut.

"Okay," I say, my voice still raspy from the tears. "Okay, I can do all of that except—Mom, I left the dress at home. It was in the—"

Mom rolls her eyes and pulls the tip of the box out of her gigantic Mom purse. I almost cry all over again, but she gives me a no-nonsense look, and I grin.

CHAPTER 36

Even though I'm wearing my dress, I still feel completely naked when I reenter the living room.

I didn't think of actually *wearing* the dress when I started drawing it in class, but it's soft against my body, and light in a way that makes me immediately think of dancing. The colors of the rainbow blend into each other, reaching my toes. It makes me want to twirl. As soon as I step down the stairs, I do, and the room breaks into applause. It's like something out of a movie.

Now that I'm inside, I can see just how much work went into decorating, and it takes a ton of strength not to let my jaw drop. Rainbow streamers hang from the walls. One side of the living room is filled with small round tables draped with white cloths, a different-colored balloon floating up at the center of each. The other side is empty, presumably for dancing.

"Holy shit," I say. I can't hide the glee in my voice. I'm on the verge of screaming. "I can't believe this is actually happening."

"Language," Mom says, but her voice is drowned out by the sound of laughter. Naomi materializes in the crowd and I practically tackle her, screaming my head off.

I'm not thinking about the fact that everyone in this room now knows that I'm bisexual and queer and I didn't have to tell them. They all showed up. They all must've helped. That means something—it means that this isn't going to be a battle. I want to grin and cry and scream all at the same time. But the tears come out first. Jesus, I'm crying more than a soap star.

"Stop *crying*," Naomi says into my shoulder. She sounds like she might cry, too. "We wanted to do something nice. You're not allowed to be sad, okay?"

She squeezes me and I squeeze her back.

"I'm not sad," I say. "I'm really happy. I didn't think I'd be able to . . ."

My voice trails off. How do I explain this to her when I'm still soaking in every single detail of this party? The whole thing looks like a rainbow threw up—and I love it. Everyone is wearing different colors, blue and red and purple. Even Mom is wearing a yellow shirt, something I didn't notice before we left. A cluster of my classmates linger by a long table of food—rainbow bagels and macaroons and normal party food like chicken tenders and potato skins.

The song has changed since I was upstairs putting on my dress, and now Mr. and Mrs. Sanders are practically grinding to "No Diggity" by Blackstreet. In the corner, Mom and Jada chat like old friends, the kids huddled close by. Avocado Man—Jimmy—wearing an actual suit jacket, stands near the food table and talks to Cal while they eagerly explain something.

"I can't believe you invited him," I say. "I can't believe he came."

"He was really nice about it," Naomi says. "And I think he

bought you a present, even though he was confused about what this was for."

It feels like a dream.

My dad is the only one who isn't here. There's a small twinge of disappointment I can't ignore. But when I look out at the party—at the dancing, at the sea of faces belonging to people I love—it all feels like enough. I may not be able to count on my dad to change, but my life definitely isn't empty without him.

I'm about to head to the dance floor when Siobhan appears in front of me. She's holding some sort of rainbow cape with a shy smile on her face.

"I'm supposed to make you wear this," she says. "But then I'd miss how pretty you look in that dress."

My cheeks heat.

"Oh," I say. "Hi."

"That's not a witty line, Mahalia," Siobhan says. "When I say something witty, you're supposed to come up with a clever comeback—"

I cup her face in my hands and kiss her.

"Um," Naomi says. "I think I need to get more ice. Cody!"

He appears immediately at his name, holding out his hand. She takes it, shooting me an *Oh my God* kind of look as he pulls her toward the dance floor.

"I'm sorry," Siobhan says when I pull away. "For ignoring you, and then singing at you—"

"I loved it," I say. "I mean, not the other part, but I know why you did it. I loved the singing."

"I thought you might," she says, suddenly shy. "I'm glad you liked it."

"Are you okay with it, though?" I ask, taking her hand in mine. "That, like, people know?"

After our impromptu performance yesterday, videos started appearing on Instagram and Snapchat. It's only gone moderately viral—most of the comments are from students in our district and the surrounding area—mostly because the video quality is so bad. But even though we didn't formally announce ourselves as a couple, serenading each other in front of the junior class leaves little to the imagination.

"I think so," she says. "I realized . . . I *was* scared for people to know. But I was more scared that Danny would take that away from me. That he would twist this really excellent thing into something ugly. Does that make sense?"

"Absolute sense." I squeeze her hand. "I'm glad we got to do it our way."

She swipes her thumb against my cheek.

"Yeah," she says. "Me too."

Then she kisses me once again, for good measure. It must last for a while because we don't come up for air until Mom appears next to me and makes a sound like she's choking.

"Oh, Mom, this is Siobhan," I say. "Siobhan, this is my mom."

This day is already so perfect—I'm praying introducing them to each other won't mess it up. To my delight, Mom pulls Siobhan in for a hug. I don't care that it lasts for less than thirty seconds and that she gives Siobhan the most awkward smile imaginable, like she's one of the elderly white people she used to take care of. It's so much more than I expected.

"Siobhan," Mom says, pronouncing her name perfectly. "I've heard so much about you."

After they've introduced themselves, I pull Siobhan to the center of the room, where Naomi and I try our hardest to teach her how to floss. She looks like she's hula-hooping.

"It's because she's Irish," Naomi says, yelling to be heard over Lil Nas X's "Thats What I Want." "I don't think they have any rhythm."

"I resent that!" Siobhan's mom calls from across the room.

Siobhan holds my hand as we try our best to dance to the same beat. I notice Mom looking at me from across the room. I'm expecting something—I don't know what. Maybe for her to touch the cross sitting around her neck, to narrow her eyes, to tell me to stop making a scene. But she gives me a smile, almost shy, like I'm someone she just met and is trying to impress. I grin back at her.

And then I kiss Siobhan. I touch her hair and her face and hear the sound of someone going "Whoa" in the background. I'm pretty sure it's Naomi's dad. But I don't care. Society might expect me to come out over and over again, but this party has taught me that it can be a moment of joy, a way to celebrate myself. Coming out can be something I do just for me.

JUNE

CHAPTER 37

"Mahalia is basically an old man."

"If having good taste in music means I'm an old man, then so be it," I say.

Prince is currently blaring on the radio. Every time Naomi moves to change the station, I jump forward and slap her hand away. Siobhan just shakes her head at us and climbs in next to me.

"You two," she says, "are absolutely ridiculous."

She waves at her house before Naomi pulls away from the curb and heads in the direction of our school. When Naomi first started driving us all to school—with Siobhan and me in the back together—she said she felt like she was driving Miss Daisy. Now I guess she embarrasses me in front of Siobhan to make up for it. To be honest, I don't really care.

It's June, the last week of school, and all I can think about is summer. Naomi and I will work together at Greta's during the week and take a free SAT class at the library on Wednesdays. Mr. Willis said he'd email me different scholarship opportunities he hears about—ones that *don't* require SAT scores. I'm still waiting for his notes on my first draft of an essay.

"'How My Coming-Out Party Changed My Life,'" he read when I plopped it on his desk. "I didn't peg you for a debutante."

I just grinned and walked away. He honestly had no idea.

In between all my summer activities, there will be time with Siobhan—at the beach, at her house, at her new job at the local outdoor gear store. I don't think I've ever been so excited for a summer before. Even now, just sitting here with Siobhan, I can't help but angle my body at her like I'm a flower and she's the sun.

Naomi glances back at us in the rearview mirror and sticks out her tongue at me.

"Mahalia has a crush on Prince," Naomi says. "So we aren't allowed to listen to anything else."

"Not exactly," I say. "Because, like, he's no longer with us on this astral plane. But have you seen him in the 'When Doves Cry' music video? Like, in the leather jacket and everything? With his smolder?"

I let out a nervous giggle. Siobhan doesn't stop smiling. I can't tell if it's because she feels bad for me or if she finds me hilarious or a little bit of both.

"I mean," Siobhan says. "Who *doesn't* have a crush on Prince?"

"Oh my God," Naomi says, smacking her hands against her steering wheel. "You're just as bad as her. I'm ignoring you both."

"Whatever," I say. "I'm used to being ignored. Siobhan ignores me when I start talking about the Police."

"No offense," Siobhan says. "But . . . maybe you need to widen your musical taste."

I gasp. Naomi cackles.

"See!" she says. "Your girlfriend agrees with me."

I lean back in my seat. Whenever anyone uses the g-word,

I'm knocked out for a few seconds and start grinning like a maniac. *Girlfriend.* Siobhan is my *girlfriend.* I eat dinner at her house on Fridays and we hold hands in the hallways and I can kiss her whenever I want. *Girlfriend.* God, I love her.

"Oh no," Naomi says. "She's got that look in her eye."

Siobhan giggles and presses a kiss to my cheek. I want to kiss her for real, but I know that if we start, we won't be able to stop. Or, more accurately, *I* won't want to stop. And as much as I tease her, it wouldn't be fair to Naomi to be ignored while her friends are making out in her backseat.

"I don't mind," Siobhan says, more to me than Naomi. "I like that look."

"Ew," Naomi says. "No offense."

"I *am* offended," I say. "You can't stop love, Naomi."

"Yeah," Siobhan says. "I'm trying to flirt here."

"I don't think you have to flirt," I say, leaning forward. "I'm already into you."

"Oh God," Naomi says, turning on her signal. "I'm glad I don't have to watch this. You have three minutes until we're at school."

I'm glad we're in the back. It's just the two of us, even if Naomi keeps making noises in the front seat. I can't help but smile. My two favorite people and me and *kissing.* What could be better?

ACKNOWLEDGMENTS

It takes a ton of people to put a book together, and I want to thank everyone at Knopf, Random House, and Penguin UK for all of their hard work on this book. Without you, the cover wouldn't be as gorgeous as it is, the book's timeline would make completely no sense, and the book wouldn't have made it this far in the first place. I'm forever indebted to you all.

My agent, Beth Phelan, always has to come near the top of this list. Thank you for answering my shady and anxious texts promptly, even when they should probably go ignored, and for all of your excitement for this idea and many others that never came to light. As Cuba Gooding Jr. says in *Jerry Maguire*, "You are my ambassador of quan" (whatever that means).

I'd also like to thank my amazing family and my awesome friends, including but not limited to Joelle, Christina, Michael, CJ (for your gay expertise), Anna, Katie, Parmida, Shelly, Mish, Cody, and Jake. You're all saints for putting up with me.

I'm also extremely grateful to other authors who read early copies of this book and shared kind words or blurbed, including Jasmine Guillory, Rachael Lippincott, Meryl Wilsner, Victoria

Lee, Mason Deaver, Becky Albertalli, and Emery Lord. I love your books and am so honored that you took the time to read and support the book!

I wrote the first draft during my last year of high school, which feels like a completely different era. I still have to thank my teachers, especially those from 2018 and the ones from college, which I graduated from while working on this book. Thank you to Ms. Kalter for letting me use your classroom like a Starbucks to write in. And thank you to all of my professors who not only forced me to learn plot structure (ugh) but also supported my creativity, pushed me, and let me brag a little bit during office hours, especially Professor Sanders, who encouraged me to write a screenplay adaptation of this book before he even set eyes on it.

Writing a book with two girls falling in love has been really difficult for me. I felt like I was a fraud and a fake, and like I wasn't queer enough to do this. For a long time, I had a hard time finding YA books with two girls falling in love, so I want to thank authors who wrote my favorite examples of this and made me feel like f/f books could be fun and flirty and romantic, including Jaye Robin Brown, Nina LaCour, Emily M. Danforth, Ciara Smyth, Leah Johnson, and Adiba Jaigirdar.

And last but certainly not least, I want to thank every single bookseller, blogger, tweeter, librarian, TikToker, and reader who has picked up any of my books. Any time I'm tagged in a post about one of my books, I'm reminded that my books exist outside of myself, and people are picking them up. I'm beyond grateful for you sharing the books, talking about them, reading them, or borrowing them. I couldn't be an author without any of you and I will never forget it.

image copyright © Louisa Wells

Camryn Garrett was born and raised in New York. In 2019, she was named one of Teen Vogue's 21 Under 21 and a Glamour College Woman of the Year. Her first novel, *Full Disclosure*, received rave reviews from outlets such as *Entertainment Weekly*, the *Today* show, and the *Guardian*, which called a 'warm, funny and thoughtfully sex-positive, an impressive debut from a writer still in her teens'. Her second novel, *Off the Record* received three starred reviews. *Friday I'm in Love* is her third novel. Camryn is also interested in film and recently graduated from NYU's Tisch School of the Arts. You can find her on Twitter @dancingofpens, tweeting from a laptop named Stevie.

PRAISE FOR *OFF THE RECORD*

'Brave, necessary, and unflinchingly real, *Off the Record* is an instant classic.'
MARIEKE NIJKAMP, *This Is Where It Ends*

'Part thriller, part rom-com, and an altogether empowering intersectional takedown of privilege, systemic complicity, and sexual assault.'
CHRISTINA HAMMONDS REED, *The Black Kids*

'Thoughtful and incisive – Camryn Garrett's voice comes through in beautiful clarity.'
RORY POWER, *Wilder Girls*

'This fresh, engrossing read will appeal to fans of Garrett's debut novel, *Full Disclosure*, as well as those new to her fast-paced prose, wit, pitch-perfect dialogue, and memorable characters. An irresistible, unapologetically feminist story.'
KIRKUS, Starred Review

'*Off the Record* is a timely and powerful story about finding the courage to use your voice to break oppressive silences.'
RANDY RIBAY, *Patron Saints of Nothing*

'A powerful, compulsive story of #metoo, speaking up, speaking out, and confronting injustice. Garrett's book is a timely, brave, and much needed story.'
KATHLEEN GLASGOW, *Girl in Pieces*

PRAISE FOR *FULL DISCLOSURE*

'Camryn Garrett has penned an unflinchingly honest, eye-opening, heartful story that's sure to keep readers talking.'
ANGIE THOMAS, *The Hate U Give*

'*Full Disclosure* is romantic, funny, hopeful, and unflinchingly real, with some next-level theater kid geekery to boot.'
BECKY ALBERTALLI, *Simon vs the Homo Sapiens Agenda*

'Mind-blowingly powerful, *Full Disclosure* is an intense, unapologetically sex-positive read . . . A book I wish I'd had growing up.'
SANDHYA MENON, *When Dimple Met Rishi*

'Fearless and affirming, *Full Disclosure* is a celebration of love, friendship, and being true to yourself.'
MARIEKE NIJKAMP, *This Is Where It Ends*